A Cry For Help

✪ ✪ ✪

Dear Sam,

I hope this reaches you. I would not write, but we—my husband, Jack, and I—are desperate. There is trouble in the Basin, and if we do not receive help soon, we will lose the ranch. We may lose our lives, as well.

I have no one else to turn to, Sam. Come, please, if you can. I repeat, we are desperate.

Your cousin,
Lucinda

Sam lowered the letter. So, Lucy was married. Of course she would be, after all these years. What kind of trouble was she in? It must be bad, or she wouldn't have called on him. She knew the danger involved in Sam's returning to Montana as well as he did.

Still . . . Lucy was Sam's only blood kin in the world. He could not refuse her pleas—and he would not, even if he could.

He was going to Montana.

Also by Dale Colter

The Regulator
Diablo at Daybreak
Deadly Justice
Dead Man's Ride
Gravedancer
The Scalp Hunters
Paradise Mountain
Desert Pursuit

Published by
HARPERPAPERBACKS

DALE COLTER

THE REGULATOR

MONTANA SHOWDOWN

HarperPaperbacks
A Division of HarperCollinsPublishers

HarperPaperbacks   *A Division of* HarperCollins*Publishers*
10 East 53rd Street, New York, N.Y. 10022

Cover illustration by Miro

First printing: April 1993

Printed in the United States of America

HarperPaperbacks and colophon are trademarks of HarperCollins*Publishers*

❖ 10 9 8 7 6 5 4 3 2 1

CHAPTER 1

SAM SLATER HAD NO PERMANENT ADDRESS, but he had ways of getting mail. Messages to him were usually forwarded to county sheriffs or territorial marshals, in the hopes that Sam would catch up with them in his wanderings.

On this midsummer day, Sam was in Tucson, where he had delivered the mortal remains of Joe Bedford and his son, Ezekiel, to the resident U.S. Marshal. The Bedfords had operated a way station near Globe, where they killed and robbed unwary travelers, then disposed of the bodies. When people had gotten suspicious, the Bedfords had fled. When a reward had been posted, Sam had gone after them.

Now the Bedfords were on Boot Hill, awaiting burial, and Sam was in Marshal Hiram Christiansen's office, watching the marshal count out his reward money. "Fifteen hundred," said the marshal, handing the stack of bills to Sam. "That's all of it."

Sam stuffed the money into his trousers. "Any messages for me?" he asked, almost as an afterthought.

"A few," said the marshal. He was a terse, wiry man who didn't like bounty hunters. He knelt, pulled open the bottom drawer of his file cabinet, and rummaged inside. "I wish you'd have this stuff sent somewheres else. I ain't running no post office here."

Sam grinned, as the marshal straightened and handed him a small pile of correspondence. There were wanted circulars forwarded by other lawmen, by victimized financial institutions or by relatives of the aggrieved, who hoped that Sam might take up the chase. There were also two requests from firearms manufacturers for Sam to endorse their products, as well as a request from a news monthly for a paid interview. The last three he tossed in Christiansen's trash basket. The circulars he kept.

"Oh, yeah," said the marshal. "I almost forgot. There's a letter for you, too."

"A letter?" said Sam, puzzled. Who would be sending him a letter?

The marshal went into his file cabinet again. "I been keeping that separate."

He handed the letter to Sam. As Sam took it he went cold inside, because he recognized the handwriting, though he had not seen it since he was fifteen. It was from his cousin Lucinda, in Montana.

Memories washed over him—memories of childhood adventures and sorrows. Lucinda—Lucy, he had always called her—had been like a sister to him, closer than a sister in many ways. Her father Henry had taken in Sam after his own parents had been killed in a Sioux raid. Her father, Sam's uncle. . . .

Other memories—unwanted ones—came back now, memories of that terrible night. Memories of Lucy's screams, of Sam running through the rain from the barn where he slept to the ranch house. Memories of what he had seen there in the flickering light—of his drunken uncle atop Lucy, his own daughter, ripping off her clothes, trying to force himself upon her. Sam remembered how he had tried to save Lucy. He remembered how his uncle had come at him with a knife, wild-eyed with drink and anger, slashing his face open. He remembered how he had fought back with his own knife and how he had killed his uncle, gutting him like a fish. . . .

Involuntarily, Sam touched the long, ragged scar that ran from his left ear to the corner of his mouth. He remembered how Lucy had sewn the wound closed in the dim light, with trembling fingers, and the rain and thunder in the background.

"You look like you've seen a ghost," said Marshal Christiansen.

"I have, in a way," Sam replied. "When did this come in?"

The marshal thought. "About the beginning of June, it was. Some cowhand brought it. Come down from Montana, I believe."

"Thanks," said Sam.

Sam half stumbled out of the marshal's office, into the blinding glare of the desert afternoon. He remembered how he had left Montana the morning after he had killed his Uncle Henry, riding Lucinda's favorite horse, wanted for murder, with the law hot on his tail. He had not seen or heard from Lucinda since that day. And now this letter. . . .

The letter was addressed:

"Mr. Sam Slater
Tucson, A.T.
Please forward if
whereabouts known"

Sam was usually sure of motion, but right now his fingers fumbled as he opened the envelope and unfolded the letter. It was dated last March, written in pen on a sheet of unlined paper. The script was large and careful, in the manner of a person who wrote infrequently. The spelling and punctuation were all correct, though; Lucy would have checked them. She was that way.

It read:

Dear Sam,

I hope this reaches you. I would not write, but we—my husband, Jack, and I—are desperate. There is trouble in the Basin, and if we do not receive help soon, we will lose the ranch. We may lose our lives, as well.

I have no one else to turn to, Sam. Come, please, if you can. I repeat, we are desperate.

Your cousin,
Lucinda

Sam lowered the letter. So, Lucy was married. Of course she would be, after all these years. A beautiful girl like Lucy could have had her pick of men. She probably had a half-dozen kids by now, as well. Still, it seemed strange to think of her in that way. In Sam's mind she had remained frozen in time, as he had last seen her —his childhood playmate budding into a young woman of sixteen.

What kind of trouble was she in? It must be bad, or she wouldn't have called on him. She knew the danger involved in Sam's returning to Montana as well as he did.

He let out his breath and looked around the sun-splashed street, but he did not really see anything. His mind was a thousand miles away. If he returned to Montana, he would be forced to confront his past. He was still wanted for the murder of his Uncle Henry there. In Montana, Sam would no longer be the hunter. He would be the hunted.

Still . . . Lucy was Sam's only blood kin in the world. He could not refuse her pleas—and he would not, even if he could.

He was going to Montana.

CHAPTER 2

LUCINDA'S LETTER WAS DATED LAST MARCH. It was mid-July now. Montana was about a thousand miles from Tucson, as the crow flew, and Sam was no crow. It would be September before he got there. By then—by now, even—the trouble in Arrowhead Basin could be over. Lucy could have lost her ranch. She could be dead.

At the thought of harm coming to Lucy, Sam felt his gut tighten. He wanted to leap on his horse and gallop off to help her. But the distance was too great for that kind of action, and nothing that Sam could do would shorten it. He had to prepare.

With the reward money he had gotten from bringing in the late Joe and Ezekiel Bedford, Sam bought himself a new horse and pack horse. He purchased clothes, blankets, and ammunition. He bought supplies of flour, coffee, salt, and sugar, along with a locally made pemmican. The pemmican wasn't as good as Sam could have made himself, but he didn't have time to dry meat. He would hunt fresh meat on the way when the opportunity presented itself. He allowed himself only one luxury. He spent an afternoon roaming the bottomlands around the Santa Rita River, gathering hackberries and mesquite seeds. He ground these into a paste with a bit of sugar—the sugar was his contribution to an old Apache recipe—and baked it into cakes. These mesquite cakes were a staple of the Apache trail diet, and Sam had grown to love them in his years as an adopted member of the tribe.

As soon as he was ready, he left. He spared neither himself nor his horses, which he replaced at every opportunity. His journey took him from the cactus-studded hills around Tucson, through the barren wastes of western Arizona, and across the Colorado River. There he turned northeast, through Nevada and Utah, crossing the Great Salt Lake Desert until he came to the city of the Mormons. From there, he traversed South Pass and the sagebrush-covered plains of Wyoming, turning north through the Big Horn Basin, until at last he came to the lush valleys and wooded hills of Montana. With every mile that he rode north, his heart beat faster. He recognized landmarks long forgotten. The bugling of elks in the hills sounded like a welcoming call. He felt like he was coming home.

It was September now. Ice skimmed the surface of the streams each morning, to melt off when the sun rose. The pine-green hills were swirled with gold by stands of aspen, as if by an invisible paintbrush. The days themselves were crisp, with an early autumn haze. It would not be long before the winter snows surged down from Canada.

At last Sam topped a pass in the mountains and halted. Spread below him was the Arrowhead Basin, a giant bowl surrounded by mountains, with a total area just slightly smaller than the state of Rhode Island. The Basin, and the river that fed it, had been named by Sam's father, who along with Sam's Uncle Henry had been the first white men to settle this region.

The beauty of the sight took Sam's breath away, from the sere grasses of the range land to the green and gold of the hills, to the sunlight glinting off streams and lakes, to the snowtipped peaks of the Bitterroots in the far distance.

Here and there were signs of settlement, signs that hadn't been present the last time Sam had stood at the head of this pass—the morning that he had fled the Basin after killing his uncle. There was a town now near the Basin's entrance, and ranches and farmhouses scattered here and there along the watercourses.

Sam backed his horses away from the pass. He wanted to enter the Basin by a different route, avoiding the town. He didn't want to meet anyone until he'd had a chance to speak to Lucy, if she was still here—if she was still alive.

He worked along the timbered ridges, heading gradually downward. The autumn smells of the Basin drifted up to him along with the sweet pine of the hills. He filled his lungs with the bracing air and let his mind drift, back through the years to . . .

A bullet thunked into the trunk of a lodgepole pine nearby. Sam heard the shot a half second after, but by then he was throwing himself from the saddle to the ground, pulling his Winchester from its saddle scabbard as he did.

Another bullet plowed into the ground, as Sam rolled away and scrambled behind the cover of an earthen bank. His horse and pack horse clattered down the hill.

Sam glanced over the bank. A wisp of smoke from a clump of boulders told him where the shooter was, above him and to the right. Sam fired his rifle at the spot. He had no hope of hitting anything; he just wanted to give his attacker something to think about. In response, another bullet slammed into the earthen bank nearby. Sam fixed the muzzle flash and fired back.

Sam crawled along the earthen bank, out of sight to whoever it was that was trying to kill him. When he had gone far enough, he left the bank and padded silently upward, using the thick forest for cover.

He got to a position above the shooter's and moved toward the clump of rocks. He was almost there when he heard the thudding sounds of a horse, jogging away. He ran forward into the rocks, to find his assailant gone. The sound of the horse receded through the trees. It was useless to consider pursuit in this country.

Sam searched around the rocks and found three spent .44–40 shells, along with the boot prints of whoever it was that had been shooting at him. He went back down the hill. His hat had come off when he dove from the horse. He picked it up, beat the dirt off, and put it back on. Then he started after his horse and pack horse.

"Welcome home," he said to himself.

CHAPTER 3

IT WAS CLOSE ON NOON WHEN SAM CAME out of the hills. He rode across the Basin, crossing the Arrowhead River at a remembered—and little used—ford. The land was open, lonely. Sam saw no one, only occasional grazing cattle. He turned up a stream, following it northeast, toward the purple hills that surrounded the Basin. At last he saw a ranch on the stream's far side.

Sam reined in. The autumn sunlight sparkled off the stream like millions of diamonds. Sam sat his horse, staring through the watery haze. It was like looking back in time.

The old log cabin of his memory was gone. In its place was a snug frame cottage with a stone chimney, except for its wide porch more nearly resembling a New England fisherman's home than a ranch house. There were more outbuildings now, as well. Everything was neat and well maintained, but somehow the ranch lacked the look of prosperity.

The dogs had caught wind of him, and they ran to the stream's edge, barking. Sam paid them no attention. In his mind's eye he saw a young boy riding across the range toward the house, happy, blond hair flying behind him.

Then the vision dissolved, as a figure appeared at the ranch house door, attracted by the barking dogs. It was a woman, carrying a rifle. The woman stared at Sam for a minute, then she lowered the rifle. She seemed to go weak at the knees, so that she had to hold onto the door jamb to keep from falling.

Sam nudged his horse across the stream. The woman at the front door recovered her composure. She stepped off the porch into the sunlight. Sam halted his horse before her and dismounted.

"Sam?" she said. Her voice was almost a whisper.

"Hello, Lucy."

They gazed at each other for a moment, taking each other in, as if trying in these few seconds to make up for all the lost years. The promise of Lucinda's youth had been fulfilled by her beauty as a grown woman. She might almost have been Spanish, with the jet-black hair that she wore straight back from an oval face. She had naturally red lips and wide-set, lavender eyes under arched brows. Her simple blouse and gray skirt only highlighted her beauty.

"It's been a while," Sam said.

"It's been too long," Lucinda replied. Then she threw herself into Sam's arms and kissed him, her hot tears dripping down his cheek and neck.

"Oh, Sam, is it really you? I thought I'd never see you again."

They stood back, holding each other's hands. Sam was smiling now. Lucinda looked at the long scar on his cheek. Tentatively, sniffing back her tears, she reached out and touched it.

"I didn't do a very good job with that, did I?"

Sam remembered how she had sewn the terrible wound shut, in the dim light with her father dead in the room beside them and the rain and thunder all around, unnerved by the shock of what she had been through. Even now, he marveled at how she had managed to remain calm through the procedure and he remembered the touch of her hands, skilled beyond their years. "I think you did just fine, Lucy."

She hugged him again, sighing, burying her

face in his chest. "Oh, Sam. You look so different than I imagined. You've changed."

"It's been a long time since I left, Lucy. A lot's happened."

"I'm just so glad you're here. I didn't think you would come. I really didn't think my letters would get to you."

"How many did you send?"

She laughed; she still had that same musical laugh. "Ten. Where did you get yours?"

"Tucson."

"Tucson." She repeated the word. It was only a name to her; it had no meaning. It might have been the far side of the moon for all she knew about it. She said, "I told Lee—that's Lee Nelson, the cowboy who worked for us—to drop one at every big town he passed through, hoping one of them would get to you. Lee was from Texas. He rode for us a couple years, then headed back south because he couldn't abide any more of these Montana winters, and because . . . well, because of other reasons, too. It was funny—coincidence, really. It was right before Lee left us. We were talking about the trouble here, and I said, 'I wish my cousin, Sam Slater, was still here to help us.' 'Not *the* Sam Slater?' Lee said, and I said, 'Don't tell me you know him?' He laughed and said everybody from his part of the country knew about Sam Slater. He said you were a . . . a bounty hunter?"

"That's right."

"He said they even had a name for you—the Regulator?"

"All bounty hunters are called regulators," Sam explained. "I just seem to be more well known than the others."

She shook her head. "I always pictured you settled down by now, with a family."

"I guess I'm not the settled-down type."

"I'm sorry."

Sam shrugged.

Lucinda stepped away. "Well, here, let's turn your horses into the corral, then you come inside. Are you hungry? You always did like to eat."

Sam grinned. "I'm famished. I'm also tired of my own cooking."

Lucy helped Sam unsaddle his horse and pack horse. She was as skilled with animals as any man. As Sam draped his saddle over a corral pole, he said, "Where's your husband? You know, I just realized—I don't even know what your last name is now."

She laughed again. "It's Mitchell. Jack's visiting the other ranches in the Basin, calling an emergency meeting of the Independent Stockmen's Association—he's the president." She grew serious. "Sam, I can't tell you how much I appreciate your coming. I know how dangerous it is for you to be in Montana again."

"Seems like it's dangerous for everybody,

these days. Somebody took a few shots at me as I rode in."

"It could have been anyone, that's how bad things are. It could have even been someone on our side, thinking you were Chandler's new gunman."

"Chandler?"

"Clay Chandler. He's the biggest rancher in the Basin. It's because of him we're having all the trouble. Come on, I'll tell you about it over lunch."

They went inside the cottage. There were just four rooms—parlor, kitchen, dining area, and bedroom. Sam stopped and looked around. The smells, the furnishings—nothing was as he remembered. The furniture was store bought, a far cry from the handmade items of Sam's youth. There were curtains on the windows and rugs on the floors, not the old grain sacking that Sam remembered. The flooring itself was of sanded and varnished pine, instead of the log cabin's packed earth. Everything was spotlessly clean, making Sam conscious of how dirty and unkempt he was. While he took a seat at the table, Lucinda poured him coffee from a pot kept heating on the stove.

"How long have you been married?" Sam asked her.

"Three years."

"No kids?"

"No. No children."

"But you're happy?"

"Happy? Oh, yes. Of course."

"And all those years before you got married, you ran this place by yourself?"

"I tried to."

"Good looking as you are, I'm surprised it took you so long to get married."

"I guess I never met the right man."

"I bet plenty of 'em asked you, though."

"A few."

Lucinda set fresh bread and butter on the table, along with a jar of homemade gooseberry jam, while she carved a cold ham from the pantry. Sam slathered jam on the bread and munched it down.

"So tell me about this Chandler," he said.

"Clay owns the Lazy H Ranch on Bear Creek. He came to the Basin a few years after you left, with a small herd he brought up from Texas. He was well liked at first. He was hard working, a good neighbor. We still had trouble with the Indians in those days, and Clay was always the first to help. But then he changed. As his herd grew, so did his ambition. He wanted more and more land, more grazing room. He bought out—or ran out—his neighbors, but that wasn't enough. Now he wants the whole Basin for himself."

Sam whistled. "The whole Basin? That'd make him as big a cattle king as any in Texas."

"That's his goal—and he'll do anything he can to reach it."

"Such as?"

Lucinda finished slicing the ham and set it on the table. "Threats, poisoned water holes, murder. The Basin's been plagued by rustlers. Every spread's been hit, but Clay's, being the biggest, has been hit worst of all. He says it's the small ranchers who are stealing his cattle."

"But aren't the small ranchers being hit, too?" Sam asked.

"That doesn't mean anything to Clay. There's no law here, so he's taken the law into his own hands. He's sworn to exterminate every rustler in the Basin. That's . . . that's why I sent for you. Clay accuses Jack of being the rustlers' leader."

"Is he?" Sam asked.

"Sam, how can you ask such a thing?"

"I have to know what I'm getting into."

"No, he isn't the leader. He formed the Independent Stockmen's Association to fight Chandler. That's why Clay's against him."

Sam looked at her with sharp eyes. "That the only reason Chandler's against him?"

Lucinda hesitated. "All right. Clay Chandler is, or was, in love with me. He asked me to marry him years ago. He's never forgiven me for turning him down. Then, when I married Jack, Clay turned his anger on him."

Sam nodded, understanding.

She went on. "Since the first of the year, two of our riders have been killed. Nobody knows who did it."

"But you think it was Chandler?"

She nodded. "Our other hands have quit and either left the Basin or gone to work for Chandler. It's the same all over. Most of the small ranchers have either been killed, sold out, or just run away. There's only a few of us left, and we can't hold out much longer. The fall roundup starts in a few weeks, and Clay's told the small ranchers he doesn't want them taking part until he's finished. He's claiming all the mavericks and unbranded yearlings in the Basin for his own. That's bad enough, but if we don't take part in the roundup, Clay will put the Lazy H brand on everything with horns—no matter how old it is or what brand it was wearing when he started."

"Will you sell out?"

Lucinda shook her head. "Jack doesn't scare easily. He's stubborn. He swears he'll go down fighting. Chandler's payroll is already stacked with long riders. I'd say half his men are there for other reasons than to work cattle. Now we've learned that he's hired a killer out of Deadwood. We don't know the man's name, or even if he's in the Basin yet. Jack wants to hold our roundup early, to get a jump on Chandler.

That's why he's called the meeting of the Stockmen's Association."

"And if you have this early roundup?"

"Chandler will try to stop us."

"Sounds like a recipe for war," Sam said.

"That's what it will be, Sam. It'll be war, and we won't stand a chance."

Sam said, "Maybe I should have a talk with this Chandler."

"He's not the kind of man you can talk to . . ." She saw the look on his face. "What is it?"

Sam had half turned his head. "Someone coming."

Lucinda listened. "I don't hear anyone."

Sam smiled. "It's a trick I picked up from the Apaches. The dogs aren't barking, so they must know whoever it is."

Sam stood and walked to the door, followed by Lucinda. In the distance, coming from the south along the stream, they saw a rider.

"You heard him that far off?" Lucinda marveled.

Sam laughed. Then he said, "Recognize him?"

"Of course I do. It's my husband, Jack."

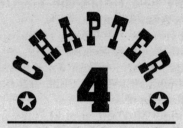

CHAPTER 4

THE RIDER APPROACHED SLOWLY, TAKING note of the two new horses in the corral. He came up to the ranch house and dismounted. He was a square-built, square-jawed man, with brick-red, curly hair and a shaggy mustache. He wore a corduroy coat, along with the low-crowned hat and woolly angora chaps favored by northern cattlemen. Sam noticed that his cheeks and the tip of his nose were thatched with broken, purplish veins.

He looked at Sam. "Who's this?" he demanded, though the tone of his voice suggested that he already knew.

Lucinda said, "This is Sam Slater, my cousin. Sam, this is my husband, Jack."

Sam stuck out his hand. "Jack."

Jack took the proffered hand perfunctorily. "Slater." He looked Sam over. "With those high-top moccasins, you could almost be an Injun."

Sam's eyes narrowed. "I lived with the Apaches for three years."

Lucinda turned to him in surprise. "Sam. I didn't know."

"I'm an adopted member of the tribe," he explained. "A blood brother, if you want to call it that."

"How . . . ?"

"After I left here, I headed south. Eventually I threw in with a freight outfit. We got jumped by Apaches in the Peloncillo Mountains. The rest of the outfit was killed, but the Apaches caught me alive. For some reason they didn't kill me. Their chief saw something in me. He liked me, and he talked the rest of them into taking me to live with them. I became his adopted son."

"Did you go on the warpath with them?" Jack asked.

"I did."

"Take any white scalps?"

"If you knew anything about Apaches, you'd know they don't take scalps."

"But you *did* make war on whites?"

"You'd do better to ask if the whites made war on us."

Jack made a deprecating noise.

Lucinda stepped between them, with a warning glance at her husband. Apologetically, she explained to Sam, "Jack didn't want me sending for you."

"We can fight our own battles here," Jack argued. "We're not like Chandler. We don't need help from outside." He glowered at Sam, then turned away. "Well, as long as you're here, you might as well come in."

Jack unsaddled his horse and turned him into the corral, then he followed Lucinda and Sam inside. He removed his spurs, then he took off his chaps and hung them behind the door, along with his shell belt, coat, and hat. He regarded the table, and Sam's half-eaten meal on it, with obvious disapproval. It was as if he felt superseded by Sam's arrival.

"Drink?" he asked Sam.

"All right."

Jack lifted a chair's seat cushion and from the chair's false bottom he produced a gallon jug of whiskey. The level in the jug was well down. Taking glasses from the sideboard, Jack poured two stiff drinks and handed one to Sam.

"Thanks," Sam said.

Jack tossed down half his drink in one gulp. "I believe in making myself plain, Slater. I know all about you. I've heard about you from the first day I came to this ranch. 'Sam Slater this,' and 'Sam

Slater that.' You've been a standard I could never measure up to—no man could. It's been like living with a ghost, and now that ghost's come back to life. I've been trying a long time to replace you in Lucinda's life, and I'm not happy about you being back, taking up where you left off."

Lucinda's brows knit. "Jack, you make it sound like Sam and I were lovers."

"Sometimes that's the way *you* make it sound, Lucinda."

Lucinda bristled, but before she could say anything, Jack went on, speaking to Sam again. "Like I said, I know all about you. I know you're a bounty hunter. I also know you're wanted for murder."

"Jack," said Lucinda, "that's not fair! Maybe the law says it was murder, but I've told you that Sam was . . ."

"I know, I know. He was defending you from your father. Your knight in shining armor. I've heard the story a hundred times—two hundred, more likely. Well, I'm looking at him, and I don't see a knight, and I don't see any armor. I see a trail bum, a man who kills for a living."

Lucinda's voice was cold. "Sam has come a long way to help us, Jack, and it's not like we can't use the help. Maybe you're too proud to show thanks, but I'm not. I want to keep this ranch."

"And a bounty hunter, a killer—is that the kind of man we should be getting to help us?"

"You forget—Sam grew up on this ranch. He's got some say in what happens to it."

Jack said nothing, and Lucinda went on, "Not only that, but he's my kin, and I won't have you talking about him that way."

Sam sat motionless at the table. "It's all right, Lucy. I'm used to it."

Jack looked from one of them to the other, then dropped the subject. "Let's eat."

He sat at the table, slicing himself hunks of the ham and bread. The dogs wandered in and out. They sniffed Sam and decided he was friendly, and Jack didn't seem to like that, either. A pot pie made from quail and vegetables grown in Lucinda's garden was cooling beside the stove. Lucinda cut it and handed out three portions. "Is your meeting set?" she asked her husband.

"Yeah," said Jack. "Between me and Mike Kennedy, we got the word spread. It's going to be on Sunday, though, not Saturday. Marty Singer's youngest girl is having a birthday Saturday, and he wants to have a family celebration. He still has to buy her presents."

"I hope he takes Tom with him if he goes into Buffalo Notch."

"He said he would. I found out more about Chandler's new gun hand, by the way. Sid Allison heard that he's called Branko."

"Branko?" said Lucinda. "Is that his first name or his last name?"

"It could be his middle name for all I know," Jack replied. He looked at Sam. "That handle mean anything to you?"

Sam shook his head. "Nope."

To her husband, Lucinda said, "Do you think the rest of the ranchers will go for the early roundup?"

"If they don't, they might as well pack up and move out of the Basin now."

"It'll be dangerous. Chandler will try to stop us."

Jack finished his drink and poured another. "We don't have a choice, Lucinda. Chandler has us up against the wall either way."

There was a period of strained silence while they ate. At last Sam said, "You've fixed the place up nice, Lucy."

"That was mostly Jack," Lucinda explained. "He's good with his hands. He can build just about anything."

Across from her, Jack glowered.

"How's the spread doing?" Sam asked.

"It *was* doing quite well," she told him. "At one point we had over a thousand head. Now we're down to about six hundred—I'm not really sure what the number is. There aren't any hands to keep track of them. We should get a better idea after the roundup."

Sam nodded, drifting back into his memories again. "My father and yours brought the first cattle into this Basin. There wasn't any market for them then. We just lived on hope."

"The market's in Miles City now," Lucinda told him. "That's the nearest railhead. We drive our cattle there once a year, after the fall roundup, or sell them to professional trail bosses on consignment. There's talk of the railroad coming through to Billings, and eventually to Buffalo Notch. That's what we're all waiting for. Then we'll be able to ship our beef direct. It'll be the making of this Basin—that's if there's any of us still around to enjoy it."

When supper was finished, Lucinda cleaned off the dishes, and the three of them sat in the small front room, by lamplight. Jack continued to drink. After a while, he put down his glass and stood, weaving slightly. "I'm going to bed," he told Lucinda. "You coming?" It was almost a challenge.

"Not yet," she replied. "Sam and I have a lot to talk about."

"That's what I thought," Jack said. He stomped into the bedroom, slamming the door behind him.

Sam and Lucinda stepped outside, onto the porch. Overhead the stars shone in their millions. A chill had descended on the Basin; there would be frost before morning. Lucy pulled her shawl close around her shoulders.

"How many times have we stood here like this?" Sam wondered. "Looking at the stars?"

"I remember the time you tried to count them," Lucy said. "Till you realized you couldn't count past twelve."

Sam laughed. "We'd be out here freezing, and your pa'd be in the house with his jug, drinking himself to sleep, and we'd have to carry him to bed."

He gave her a pointed look. Lucinda understood its meaning.

"Don't be too hard on Jack," she said. "He's a good man when he isn't drinking. He's a hard worker, and he'd do anything for me. It's funny, but he didn't drink when I first met him—or no more than any man does. It's just this . . . this country. It changes a man. It's so big and lonely, especially during those long winters. There's nothing to do. Men start to drink out of boredom. It becomes a habit, then an obsession; and one day it's taken control of their lives, and they don't know how it happened. I've tried to get Jack to stop, but it's no good. He doesn't even know he has a problem." She sighed. "My father was the same way."

"I know," said Sam softly. "How'd you meet Jack, anyway?"

"He showed up one day, looking for work. He was a cowboy, up from Kansas. He'd heard about Montana and wanted to see it. There weren't many men able to work for me in those days.

After . . . after what happened with my father, I didn't like men. I didn't trust them, and I'd drive them off after a little while. I figured Jack would be the same way. I rode him hard, but he put up with me. Then, one day, I realized that he wasn't bad, that he could be trusted. We became friends. Later, we fell in love and got married."

The two of them talked long into the night, as they had done many times before, ignoring the cold. Sam told Lucinda about his life with the Apaches, and about the years since his Apache family had been killed by the army, leaving him on his own once more.

"What made you become a bounty hunter?" Lucy asked.

Sam leaned against the awning post. "I had to do something with my life. Manhunting's what I'm good at."

"Do you enjoy it?"

"Yes," he confessed, "I do. Maybe it has to do with my 'power.' "

"'Power'?"

Sam looked away, into the darkness of the basin. "Apaches believe that some people have powers given to them by the supernatural. Powers can be obtained in different ways. They can be purchased from someone who already has them, or they can come in a vision, like mine did, or in a dream. My Apache father had the power to find ammunition—which was important to our band, because we were always short. My mother had the power of healing. Other men may have power over horses, or the power of running."

"And what is your power?" Lucinda sounded like she was afraid to find out the answer.

"We call it *inda ke-ho-ndi*, 'power against enemies.' It's the strongest power there is. You'd call it the power of war, of killing. It's my gift." He laughed softly. "Some gift."

"And you're happy in that kind of life?"

"Happy? No, I don't think I'll ever be happy. I'm alive, and that's about as much as I can ask for."

They were quiet for a moment, then Sam said, "It's getting late. We better turn in. Do I get my old room in the barn?"

"No. Put your gear in the bunkhouse. You'll find firewood by the stove." Lucinda took Sam's hands. "Sam? Thank you for coming."

Sam nodded. "Tomorrow I'll go see Chandler."

"No," she said. "Tomorrow you and I will go riding, like we used to. There's going to be trouble here. Let's have one pleasant day before it starts."

"All right." Sam bent and kissed her forehead. "Good night, Lucy."

"Good night, Sam." She turned away, letting go of his hands reluctantly, and went back inside the house.

Sam stood outside in the cold for a few minutes, staring at the door, then he walked slowly to the bunkhouse.

CHAPTER 5

MARTY SINGER DROVE HIS BUCKBOARD along the rutted track that served as a road from Buffalo Notch. He had gone into town to buy birthday presents for his youngest girl, Debbie, who would be four on Saturday. The wrapped presents were under a tarpaulin in the buckboard's rear, to keep the dust off them and to hide them from Debbie when he got home. Included among them was a hobby horse that Marty had ordered from the Montgomery Ward catalogue several months before.

Marty was thirty, of medium height and average looks, with a cattleman's shaggy mustache.

He had gone into town alone, against everyone's advice. His younger brother, Tom, had planned to go with him, but he had come down sick. Marty had been scared, but he loved Debbie and he wasn't going to let anything keep him from getting her presents. Some of Clay Chandler's men had been in town, as Marty had feared they might be, but they hadn't bothered him. Now Marty felt good—and more than a little relieved—as he guided his two-horse team back across the rolling Montana plain, under the great blue bowl of a sky. There was a bite in the wind; before long this range would be covered with snow. Marty looked around, whistling cheerfully to himself. People back East couldn't grasp how big this country was—how empty it was—till they'd seen it in person. It was nearly a half-day's ride to town, and Marty lived a lot closer than some.

Marty and his brother had come to the Arrowhead Basin as homesteaders. Marty had brought his wife and children with him. He'd quickly learned that he didn't have a knack for farming, so he'd turned to cattle raising. This was back when cattle were being imported in large numbers from Texas. The long-horned cattle, half wild to begin with, had thrived on the lush Montana grasses. There were no fenced ranges, so the cattle had run loose and bred indiscriminately, and men had helped themselves to anything without a brand—and some with brands—in order to build up their herds. Marty had started that way, so had Clay Chandler and just about every other cattleman in the Basin, but those freewheeling days were past. The trick now was to hold on to what you had, to build through breeding and not let the rustlers and night riders wipe you out. Marty was a small rancher; his ambitions had never run to anything else. He wasn't yet to the point where he could call himself prosperous—though he'd had some good years when the price of beef was high—but he was getting there.

There was one man in the Basin with ambitions, however—big ones. And now Clay Chandler was accusing Jack Mitchell and the other small ranchers of stealing his cattle. Worse, he was claiming all of this fall's mavericks and unbranded yearlings as his own, to make up for what he said had been taken from him. No one expected him to stop there, either. Many a full-grown steer was likely to find itself rebranded with the Lazy H before the first snow fell.

People said Clay was behind the killings and burnings that had plagued the Basin. They said he was behind the Committee of Twenty that had sent warnings to many of the small ranchers—Marty included—to get out of the Basin. Such charges were hard for Marty to believe. He had known Clay a long time. He still considered him a friend. They had shared many a campfire and pot of coffee together.

He didn't know if Clay would be a friend much longer, though. The Independent Stockmen were meeting at Jack Mitchell's house on Sunday. There would be a big jollification, a chance for widely separated families to get together. But after the good times, there was serious work to be done. Word was, Jack was going to call on the Independents to hold their roundup a week earlier than Chandler's. That was sure to cause trouble—big trouble. The sensible thing would have been for all the ranchers to go on roundup at the same time and distribute the mavericks and yearlings on the basis of herd size. That was the way they used to do it, before Clay's operation had gotten so big. But good sense seemed to have gone out of the Basin. Marty had gone to more buryings lately than he liked to think about, and a lot of his old friends had cleared out.

Marty came to the bridge over Three-Mile Creek. He was not far from home now. He had built this bridge himself. Clay Chandler had helped him. He smiled at the memory of those days. Clay couldn't be as bad as they said.

The buckboard rumbled over the bridge planking. As he crossed, Marty thought he saw a shadow move beneath the bridge. He wondered what it could have been—a coyote? A calf? A man? What would a man be doing beneath the bridge?

As he reached the far side of the creek, Marty turned on the seat to look back. There was a rifle shot. The bullet hit Marty in the back, beneath the shoulder blade, plowing deep into his chest cavity.

Marty grunted, jolted by the force of the blow. He tried to recover his balance on the seat. As he did, a second shot rang out. The bullet entered the back of Marty's skull and blew his brains out the front.

Marty slumped in the buckboard seat, letting go of the reins. The team ran away, with the buckboard jolting behind and the wrapped birthday presents crashing around beneath the tarpaulin.

CHAPTER ·6·

SAM AND LUCINDA LEFT RIGHT AFTER BREAK-
fast the next morning. Lucinda led a long-legged,
tawny gelding from the corral.

"Nice horse," Sam observed.

Lucy stroked the horse's muzzle. "This is
Honeysuckle. He's the fastest horse in the
Basin."

Sam had roped and saddled a rugged chestnut. He touched the brand on its flank. "S Bar
S—the Slater Brothers. A long time since my pa
and yours made up this brand. They had
planned to split the profits from this ranch fifty-
fifty. They had planned to make their fortunes

here. And look what happened to them. One killed by Indians, one . . ." His voice trailed off.

"As far as I'm concerned, half of this ranch is still yours, Sam," said Lucinda.

Sam grinned. "You'd probably get an argument from Jack about that."

"I'm sorry he doesn't like you."

"I been disliked before. It goes with my profession. Where is Jack, anyway? Why wasn't he at breakfast?"

She shook her head. "He rode out early. Said he was going to look for strays."

The two of them mounted and started off. "There's someplace I want to go first," Sam said.

They rode across the stream and up it about two miles. They stopped at a wide, level spot with a pine forest behind it. There was no sign of the house that had once stood here. There was nothing but two headboards on a slight rise. The legend on the headboards read: JOHN AND HOPE SLATER. KILLED BY INDIANS, followed by the date.

The graves were in surprisingly good condition. "I've kept them up," Lucinda said. "For you."

Sam stared. He remembered next to nothing about his parents. His mother he remembered only as a warm presence, his father as a bearded face who used to toss him in the air. What would he have become if they had not died? He looked around at what had been their land—his land.

Lucinda spoke softly. "They were good people, my father said."

"Yeah," agreed Sam. "All right. Let's go."

It was a beautiful autumn morning—crisp air, fluffy clouds, here and there patches of ground mist as the frost burned off. The horses cantered rhythmically along the rolling range land, skirting patches of woods. Behind them the saw-toothed Bitterroots were dusted with snow.

Lucy wore the same outfit as yesterday, with the addition of a canvas jacket and a man's wide-brimmed hat. "I feel like I'm sixteen again," she beamed, rosy cheeked.

"I just wish we were," Sam replied.

They gave their animals a good run. They watered them at a clear creek, then walked them to the top of a wooded ridge. There they stood side by side, holding the horses' reins, looking across the Basin toward the distant Arrowhead River.

"Remember this spot?" Lucy said, with a mischievous glint in her eye.

Sam thought. "Of course! This is where we had that picnic. And we ran into the party of Blackfeet."

Lucy laughed.

Sam went on. "I was—what?—ten. I remember I was about as scared as it's possible for a body to be, but I tried hard not to show it."

"Lucky for us they were friendly. A few pieces of cold chicken, and they went on their way."

Sam shook his head, thinking of that time. "I guess you don't see many Indians these days?"

"No. They've mostly been chased up into Canada by the army. Now and then a party of the poor devils sneak off with a few cattle or pass through the Basin, but their time is gone."

They were silent for a moment. Then Lucinda sighed, as if she knew a rare contentment standing here with Sam. "I was in bad shape for a long time after you left, Sam—for years. I couldn't forget what my father tried to do to me. I blamed all men for his actions. I thought they were all like him—all except you. But you were gone, and I had no one to turn to."

"I guess it was rough, running the ranch by yourself."

"There were times I thought it was impossible. I had to sell off a lot of the stock just to keep going. I couldn't work them by myself. I hired hands, but none of them ever stayed with me long, because I couldn't get along with men."

"Is that why you turned down Clay Chandler?" Sam asked.

"No, there was more to it than that. Clay really loved me, but it would never have worked out with him. Clay is from the old school. He believes a woman should be dependent on her man, subservient to his wishes. I'm not that kind of woman—you know that. I value my freedom, my independence. I wouldn't have been much more than a slave with Clay—a spoiled and pampered slave, maybe, but a slave just the same."

She sighed again. "In some ways I feel responsible for all the trouble in the Basin. It was right after I turned Clay down that he developed this obsessive ambition to control everyone and everything around him. Sometimes I think he's doing it all to impress me, to somehow get even with me. Even the way he's accused Jack of being the rustlers' leader—it's like it's aimed at me."

"Any idea who *is* stealing the cattle?" Sam asked.

"I know it's not Jack. Clay says he's tracked stolen cattle to our range, but that's impossible."

"One of the other small ranchers, maybe?"

"It could be, but we all lose stock, just like Clay. Face it, no one is above appropriating a few strays now and then—that's part of the cattle business—but rustling on the scale that's . . . " She stopped. "What is it?"

Sam had stiffened. His eyes narrowed as he stared up the creek that ran along the bottom of the hill. He pointed. "Look there, just past that bend in the creek."

Lucinda's vision was partly obscured by the branches of intervening pines; for a moment she didn't see anything. Then she noticed movement past the bend, a bit less than a mile off, where the trees came down to the water—two animals. "It's a couple of horses grazing," she said. "Wait, they're hitched. It's a team. What's that behind them—a buckboard?"

"Looks like," said Sam. "We better check it out."

He held the bridle of Lucy's horse while she mounted, then he swung aboard the chestnut. He drew his rifle from its scabbard and levered a shell into the chamber. Then he and Lucy walked their horses down the hillside, winding their way between the pines. Sam kept a weather eye open, but there didn't seem to be anyone around.

They crossed the creek and approached the team and buckboard. Something was slumped in the buckboard's front seat, beneath a cloud of flies. It was a man.

Lucy took in her breath. "Oh, my God, I know him. It's Marty Singer—the Singers are friends of ours."

She urged her horse on, then stopped. There was black, congealed blood all over the body and the buckboard seat. The flies buzzed loudly. Maggots wriggled in and out of the dead man's shattered skull. A nauseating stench hung over the buckboard.

Lucinda worked her jaws as Sam drew up beside her. "Maybe you better not look," he said.

"No," she said stubbornly. "I . . . I need to see."

They dismounted and ground hitched their horses. Still holding the rifle, Sam climbed onto the buckboard. There was a placard around the body's neck. Sam turned the placard over, holding his breath against the smell and waving away the clouds of flies. The placard was hand painted. It read: RUSTLERS BEWARE, and it was signed: THE COMMITTEE OF TWENTY.

Sam and Lucy exchanged looks. "Marty Singer was no rustler," Lucy said angrily. "Everybody knows that. Everybody but . . ." She didn't bother to finish.

Sam looked in the buckboard's rear. Blood and brains had leaked over the seat and onto the tarpaulin. The tarp had been jolted loose in the buckboard's wild ride and had slipped part of the way off what it was covering. Gore had splattered onto some wrapped parcels, and onto a child's wooden hobby horse.

"Debbie's birthday presents," said Lucinda. "Poor Hannah. Those poor children."

Sam jumped nimbly from the wagon and began following the wagon's tracks backward through the grass. At last he squatted, Apache style, looking at something.

"What is it?" said Lucinda, coming up behind him.

Sam indicated the ground. "The killer left a print." He studied the print, which had hardened in the ground. "He's a small man, but stocky, with a wide foot. These are square heels, not from cowboy boots. The heel is worn well down on the outside." He looked up. "Sound like anybody you know?"

"No."

"Chandler? Any of his men?"

She shook her head. "None of Clay's men would be wearing boots like that."

Sam wrapped Marty Singer's body in the tarp and laid it in the rear of the buckboard. "His ranch isn't far from here," Lucinda said. "We can take the body there."

Sam tied his horse to the rear of the buckboard. Lucinda mounted Honeysuckle and led the way while Sam drove the buckboard and its grisly cargo to the Singer spread.

The Singer place was not as imposing as Jack and Lucinda's. The ranch house was small, and its sod roof had weeds sprouting from it. Marty Singer's wife, Hannah, saw them coming. At first she was excited and relieved. Marty should have been home yesterday, and when Hannah recognized Lucinda she thought Marty must have spent the night at the Mitchell place. Then she realized it was not Marty driving the buckboard.

Hannah approached the oncoming wagon, wringing her apron. Her voice was fatalistic. "They've killed Marty, haven't they?" she asked Lucinda.

As Sam reined in the team and braked the buck-board, Lucinda dismounted. She looked Hannah in the eye. "Yes, Hannah. They have." She drew the newly made widow close, trying to comfort her.

"Who done it?" Hannah said, pushing away.

"We don't know. He'd been dead for a while when we found him."

"I can guess who it was," said Hannah, her voice rising.

Just then, a little, golden-haired girl came running up from the barn. She looked in the back of the buckboard. "Look, a horsie!" she cried. "Is it for me?"

Then she noted the tarpaulin-covered bundle and its terrible smell. "What's that?"

"Come away from there, Debbie," said her mother.

"Why? What's wrong, Mamma? Where's Daddy?"

Hannah pulled the uncomprehending girl close.

"I don't understand," said the little girl. "Where's Daddy?"

Two older children appeared, a boy and a girl, attracted by the commotion. They saw the buckboard and stared. They understood what had happened. The girl started crying. The boy tried hard not to.

To Hannah, Lucinda said, "Where is Tom?" Tom was Marty's younger brother, who lived with them.

"In bed with the ague. That's why he didn't go into Buffalo Notch with Marty. If he had, maybe this wouldn't have happened."

Sam spoke up, "And if he had, maybe they'd both be dead."

The widow seemed to notice Sam for the first time. "Who is this?" she asked Lucinda.

"My cousin Sam," replied Lucinda.

A different note entered Hannah's voice. "The one we've heard about?"

"Yes."

Hannah turned to the older children. "Go inside. Take Debbie with you."

"Why, Mamma? What is it?" persisted Debbie.

"Just do as I say!"

"Go ahead," added Lucinda, ushering the little girl and her siblings toward the sod-roofed ranch house.

Softly, Sam said, "If you'll tell me where I can find a shovel, ma'am?"

Hannah shook her head. "You've done enough. Our two hands will be back soon. They can build a casket and bury him." She got a far-away look. "We'll put him on the knoll, next to Robert and James. Those are two of our children. This land killed them, too." Her voice, and her thoughts, drifted off.

"I expect you'll be having a formal ceremony later," said Lucinda, coming back.

Hannah nodded.

"We'll come."

"Thank you for bringing him. You, too, Mister . . . ?"

"Sam's good enough, ma'am."

To Sam, Lucinda said, "I'd better go into town and report this."

"There any law there?" Sam asked her.

"Just a town marshal. Chandler owns him, of course. We have to make this official, though. If we complain enough, maybe the Territorial government will help us."

"I'll come with you," Sam told her.

"Couldn't that be dangerous for you?"

"No more dangerous than it's been already."

The two of them mounted their horses and rode off, leaving the grieving Singer family in their wake.

CHAPTER 7

BUFFALO NOTCH'S SINGLE STREET WAS smeared along the south side of the Arrowhead River like a scar on the landscape. Its buildings were constructed of logs, low slung to withstand Montana's winter winds—no adobe or false-fronted frame buildings here. There were saloons, gambling halls, a few restaurants, a hotel, even a Chinese laundry. Recent rains had turned the wide street into a sea of glutinous mud, littered with empty bottles, tin cans, and enough used playing cards to float the territory's gambling industry for a year.

Sam and Lucinda rode down the street.

Wagons loaded with lumber and freight rumbled by, along with an occasional horseman. Pedestrians kept to the plank sidewalks where possible, the men's trousers tucked into high boots for protection. When they were forced to cross to the other side, they did so carefully, plucking their feet from the mud. The smells of manure, cooking food, and privies mingled uneasily in the air.

"Last time I passed this way," Sam recalled, "there was nothing here but that old mountain man's trading post. He still around?"

Lucinda said, "He stayed on for a long time, then one day he was gone—no one knew where. People said it was because he had an Indian wife, and everyone looked down on him."

Ed Cummings, Buffalo Notch's marshal, was a middle-aged, ineffectual-looking man, with an ample belly and a spreading beard. "The Committee of Twenty—looks like vigilantes at work," he opined, when Lucinda told him what had happened to Marty Singer.

"Looks like murderers to me," responded Lucinda in an acid tone.

Marshal Cummings was doubtful. "Some might call it that, I guess. Singer'd been warned to get out of the Basin. I been expectin' something like this to happen to him. I'll pass the information along to the U.S. Marshal in Helena. My writ ends at the town boundary, you know.

It's up to the Federal people what they want to do about this."

"If anything," Lucinda said bitterly.

The marshal nodded. "If anything," he agreed. He looked across the office at Sam, who was thumbing through a pile of wanted posters on the desk. "Them posters ain't for public consumption till they're posted."

Sam looked up. "Sorry."

"You're new around here," Cummings observed.

"In a way," Sam said.

"What's your business?"

Lucinda spoke up. "He's staying at our place. He's our new hand."

"Mm." Cummings scratched his beard. "Don't look much like a cowhand to me."

"Looks can be deceiving," Sam pointed out, smiling. "Some folks might say you don't look much like a marshal."

Cummings reddened and looked at Lucinda sharply. "You ain't brought in no hired gun, have you?"

"Why shouldn't we?" Lucinda said. "Clay Chandler has a couple dozen hired guns—plus that new one, Branko, we keep hearing about."

"Mm," the marshal repeated. He turned to Sam, puffing himself up. "Just make sure you keep your nose clean while you're in my town."

Sam kept smiling. "I'll do my best, Marshal."

Sam and Lucinda left the marshal's office, and Sam said, "That was a waste of time."

Lucinda said, "Why were you looking through those wanted posters?"

"I wanted to see if they had one on me."

"Did they?"

"Not that I could find."

"What you did happened a long time ago. Maybe people have forgotten."

"Maybe, but I wouldn't count on it. There's always somebody with an overactive memory."

As they returned to their horses, Lucinda remembered something. "While I'm here, I'll go down to Myerson's store and see if they have the new Butterick patterns. I promised myself a new dress this Christmas. I haven't had one in two years."

"Go ahead," Sam told her. "I'll wait here with the horses."

Myerson's dry goods store was two blocks down the street. The new patterns were not in yet—mail service from the East was terrible—so Lucinda left. As she walked out the door, she ran into three men. The men were dressed like cowboys, but something about the way they wore their guns said they'd done precious little cowboying.

"Well, looky here," said the first one, a chunky blond with a Texas accent. He doffed his hat in a mock gesture of courtesy. "We finally found us a woman in this flea-bit burg."

"Yeah," said the second. He was older than the other two, a dark, menacing type. "Good looker, too."

The third, a skinny fellow with a pock-marked face, said, "Where you work, honey?"

"If you know what we mean," added the blond, digging an elbow into the skinny fellow's ribs. The three men laughed.

The men had Lucinda's path blocked. She smelled their whiskey-soaked breaths and the rank sweat of their unwashed bodies. "I don't work anywhere," she informed them.

"Independent operator, huh?" said the blond. "That's even better."

The dark-haired man said, "You're sure a sight for these trail-weary eyes, darling. What's your name?"

"It's *Mrs.* Mitchell," Lucinda replied frostily, "and I'll thank you to stand out of my way."

The three hard cases looked at one another. "Mitchell?" said the skinny man. "You any relation to Jack Mitchell, the rustler?"

"Jack Mitchell is my husband. And he's no rustler."

The three hard cases burst out laughing. The blond said, "That ain't what we hear."

"Fancy that," the skinny man added. "This purty little thing is a rustler's wife."

"Dangerous woman," reckoned the blond with mock horror. "How 'bout taking a drink with us, Mrs. Rustler?"

The dark man added, "We got a room at Duff's Hotel. We can go over there and have us a good time."

Lucinda tried to force her way past them. "Let me by."

The men stood shoulder to shoulder, not letting her through. "Not without you give us a kiss," said the blond.

"Kiss hell," said the older one. "I want more'n a kiss from her. Rustler's woman can't afford to be particular. You come with us, darling, and make us all happy. Maybe we'll give you a few pesos for your trouble."

Lucinda stepped off the sidewalk, into the mud, to go around them. "I wouldn't go with you if . . ."

The dark man dragged her back onto the walk, squeezing her arm painfully. "I said, come with us."

Lucinda squirmed, trying to get away.

"You heard the lady," said a voice from behind them. "Let her through."

The three hard cases turned, to see Sam Slater standing on the plank sidewalk. Sam's blue eyes were like ice beneath the brim of his hat. His right hand hung easily beside his pistol butt.

"Who the hell are you?" said the chunky blond.

"Is this your husband, the rustler?" the skinny man asked Lucinda.

"Let's say I'm a friend," Sam told them.

"Hey, lookit his face," said the skinny man. "What freak show they get you out of, mister?"

"Yeah," added the blond, "where'd you get that scar?"

"I sent away for it," Sam told them. "Now, let the lady through. But before you do that, apologize to her."

"Apologize?" said the blond. "For what?"

"You got to be kidding," scoffed the skinny, pockmarked man.

The dark-haired man stared at Sam. "I don't apologize to nobody."

"Get ready to start," Sam said.

Lucinda disengaged herself from the dark man's grasp. "That's all right, Sam, it's really not . . ."

"Keep out of this, Lucy." She had never seen him like this. His eyes burned with a cold light. "Stand out of the way."

Lucinda hesitated, then backed inside the dry goods store.

Sam faced the three hard cases. "Let's hear those apologies, boys."

The three men spread out as far as they could on the narrow walk. The blond put his hat back on and stepped into the street to get a better angle of fire.

The dark-haired man said, "In case you ain't noticed, there's three of us and one of you."

"Surprise," said Sam, "you can count." Then

he smiled. "You know, where I come from, a man doesn't insult a lady. We leave that to the other women—and to cowards."

The dark-haired man snarled, "I'll show you who's a coward."

The three hard cases went for their guns.

Sam was ready. He drew his pistol smoothly, efficiently. He shot the dark-haired man first, figuring he was the most dangerous, putting a bullet squarely in his chest. His next shot went a bit high, tearing into the skinny man's throat. As the skinny man fell, Sam turned in a half crouch, firing at the chunky blond in the street, who had his own gun out by now and was firing at the same time. The blond's shot buried itself in the log wall by Sam's head; Sam's bullet hit the blond in the thigh. Before Sam could fire again, the blond dropped his gun and fell to the mud, clutching his leg and hollering with pain.

Powder smoke drifted. In the street, the wounded man was still yelling. Frightened horses and mules cried and stamped their hoofs, and passing riders had trouble controlling their mounts. People peeked from windows and doors. When they were sure the danger was past, they moved in close to see what had happened.

From the store's doorway Lucinda looked at Sam in shock. He was right, she thought; he had changed.

Eyes moving, alert for fresh danger, Sam

quickly ejected the spent shell casings from his pistol and reloaded. He stepped off the walk next to the chunky blond, who lay in the street holding his thigh, from which blood spurted, running over his trousers and mixing with the yellow-brown mud.

"Now," said Sam, "about that apology."

The wounded man looked up. "My bone is smashed, you son of a bitch. I'm going to lose this leg."

"So learn to hop," Sam told him. "Now, apologize, or I'll shoot off the other leg." He cocked his pistol and pointed it. Lucinda started to say something then thought better of it.

The wounded man grit his teeth and looked at Lucinda, sweat streaming off his face. "I'm sorry, ma'am. Didn't mean to cause you no inconvenience."

Lucinda didn't know what to say.

Sam said it for her. "The lady accepts. Thank you."

At that moment, Marshal Cummings pushed through the crowd. "What's going on here?"

Sam holstered his pistol, smiling innocently. "These boys insulted Mrs. Mitchell. I asked them to apologize, and they drew on me. I won't press charges."

Marshal Cummings looked at Sam hard. "I knew you were trouble the moment I laid eyes on you. You got any witnesses to what you say?"

"Yes," said a voice, and everyone turned as a tall man crossed the muddy street. He was a cowboy by his look, wiry and bowlegged. His jacket, hat, and loose-slung bandanna were worn and dirty. There was a day's growth of beard on his handsome face, and his brown, curly hair was turning prematurely gray.

Marshall Cummings stepped back respectfully. "These fellas work for you, don't they, Mister Chandler?"

"They *did*," said the newcomer, who looked furious with them. "I won't have men in my employ who don't know how to treat a lady. They got what was coming to them." He turned and touched his hat brim. "Are you all right, Lucinda?"

"Yes," said Lucinda, "I'm all right."

"I'd never forgive myself if anything happened to you. You know that, don't you?"

In a low voice, Lucinda replied hesitantly. "Yes, I know that."

"These were new men. My foreman must not have screened them very well. Please accept my apologies for any insult they may have given you."

"I don't want your apologies, Clay."

Behind them, Marshal Cummings directed some bystanders to remove the wounded man. "Take him to Doc Watson."

"You got a doc in this town?" Sam asked, mildly surprised.

"Horse doctor," replied the marshal.

Sam didn't envy the wounded man.

The marshal went on, in a loud voice, "Some more of you, take those dead fellows to Ross Morgan's." To Sam, he explained, "Ross is the town butcher. Does some undertaking on the side."

"Sounds about right," Sam murmured.

To the storekeeper, Marshal Cummings said, "Myerson, you'll have to clean the blood off this sidewalk—it's a civic ordinance. Makes us look bad."

The crowd broke up, but Clay Chandler stayed. Almost shyly he spoke to Lucinda. "I'm surprised to see you in Buffalo Notch."

"I came to report a murder," she told him. "Somebody shot Marty Singer on his way back from town."

Chandler raised his eyebrows. "Vigilantes?"

"Funny, that's the same thing Marshal Cummings said."

"Great minds think alike," cracked Sam.

Chandler turned. "Ah, yes, the noble savior. That was nice shooting."

"Thanks," said Sam.

Lucinda said, "Clay, this is . . ."

"Sam Slater," Chandler finished for her. "I know who he is."

"Good news travels fast," Sam remarked.

"I also know what he is," Chandler said.

"You're a bounty hunter, Mister Slater—which is kind of ironic, considering you've got a two-thousand-dollar reward on your own head."

Sam didn't bat an eye. "Maybe you'd like to try and collect it."

"I don't need the money," Chandler told him. "I understand the U.S. Marshal in Helena has been notified of your presence, however. He's no doubt on his way here after you."

"No doubt."

Lucinda looked at Sam and gripped his arm, but he said nothing. Chandler smiled pleasantly.

To Chandler, Lucinda said, "Why didn't you tell Marshal Cummings about Sam?"

The cattle king shrugged. "I like Ed, I don't want to see him hurt. The old boy'd be no match for a gunman like Slater, and he might feel duty bound to try and take him in."

"Considerate, ain't you?" Sam said.

Chandler grew earnest. "Lucinda, I'm glad you're here, because I've wanted to speak to you. Word has it your husband and his friends are planning to hold an early roundup."

Lucinda made no answer.

Chandler went on. "Let me give you some advice—don't do it. Not if you know what's good for you."

"That sounds like a threat, Chandler," said Sam.

"It's no threat, it's a statement of fact, and it's also none of your business."

"Lucinda's my cousin. I'm making it my business."

"Then you're making a mistake. This Independent Stockmen's Association, or whatever you want to call it, doesn't fool me. These people are ranchers doing a little rustling on the side, or rustlers doing a little ranching on the side—take your pick. I've lost enough stock to them, and I'm not about to lose any more. Throw in with them, Slater, and you might find yourself decorating a tree."

"Don't tell me it's Christmas already?"

Chandler grew angry, but before he could say any more, Lucinda interrupted. "We have to go," she told him.

Chandler touched her arm. "Things are coming to a head, Lucinda. Jack Mitchell and his like are bound to lose. You know, when it's all over, you could find yourself . . . free."

"Free to marry you?"

"You said it, I didn't."

"No, Clay. I don't think so."

Chandler straightened. He touched his hat brim once more. "Goodbye, Lucinda." To Sam, he nodded. "Mister Slater. I'm sure I'll be seeing you again."

"I'm looking forward to it," Sam told him.

Chandler turned away, recrossing the street. Sam and Lucinda started back to their horses. Sam glanced around warily as they walked. "How did Chandler know who I was?" he wondered.

"I don't know," Lucinda said.

"And who notified the U.S. Marshal?"

Lucinda was worried. "Sam, what are you going to do?"

"Watch my back," he said. "Not much else I can do. Everybody with a gun and a little ambition will be looking to collect that reward on me."

"Maybe you should leave?"

He looked at her. "No. There's no chance of that. Not till this is over."

CHAPTER 8

THE SUN WAS JUST RISING OVER THE PRATT ranch. The long grass was rimed white with frost.

The ranch house was made of logs, with a sod roof. Saplings planted around the front and sides would one day provide shade and a break from the northern winds. Inside, Amy Pratt was preparing Sunday breakfast, a task complicated by the fact that she carried ten-month-old Jud Junior on her hip as she worked.

The Pratts had been here for eighteen months. They were from Illinois, where newly married Judson had been enthralled by the lure of the West and had determined to become a rancher. They had homesteaded this site, and with their savings they had purchased a small herd of cattle. They had been gratified to see the herd thrive on the Montana range, though there had been trouble with their powerful neighbor, Clay Chandler, over water and grazing rights.

One handed, Amy pulled golden brown biscuits from the Dutch oven and sat them on a plate, while the baby cooed and pulled at her hair and the front of her dress. Behind her, Judson came in from the bedroom, hauling up his galluses. He was a young man, making a rather unsuccessful attempt to grow a beard. He shivered with the early morning chill as he sat at the table and poured himself a cup of coffee. The smell of frying sausage filled the small room, and he inhaled it with anticipation.

"Eat up, dear," said Amy. "We have to get an early start."

"I know, I know. We have to go to the Mitchells today. Yesterday it was the Singers, for the burying. Seems I don't never get time for work."

"Oh, Jud, you sound like an old man. Anyway, Sunday's supposed to be a day of rest."

"Only for those who can afford to rest. There's harness to be mended, and I want to get that new addition onto the house before the snow falls."

Amy was unimpressed by his reasoning. "It won't hurt Jud Junior to sleep with us a little while longer. . . ."

Outside, the dog started barking.

"Somebody coming," said Amy.

Jud sliced open a biscuit and spread it with fresh-churned butter and chokeberry jam. "Must be Matt Taverner. He said he'd ride over to the Mitchells with us."

"Funny how Matt always shows up just in time for breakfast."

Jud smiled. "You *are* a good cook, Amy. I can't blame him."

Shifting the baby on her hip—God, he was getting heavy—Amy opened the door. The dog was still barking. "Is it Matt?" asked Jud from the table.

"No. It's five men. I don't recognize them."

Jud rose and joined her in the doorway. They watched as the five men reined in before the house and dismounted, stretching saddle-stiff joints. Three of the men wore big Texas hats—a common sight in this country—and the other two were dressed like townsmen. All carried rifles and pistols. While a companion held his horse, one of the transplanted Texans stepped forward, beating dust from his clothes and doffing his hat respectfully.

"Morning, ma'am," he said to Amy. He was in his late twenties. He would have been nice looking if his teeth weren't so bad.

"Good morning," replied Amy warily.

"This the Pratt house?"

"Yes, it is. I'm Mrs. Pratt, and this is my husband, Jud." Jud nodded to the man, as Amy went on, indicating the baby on her hip, "And this is Jud Junior."

The man smiled. "Hi, little fellow," he said, holding out a finger for the baby to grab. Then he grew serious, putting his hat back on. "Mister Pratt, I'm Deputy U.S. Marshal Harold Thomas. From Helena. I've got a warrant for your arrest."

Amy and Jud looked at each other, stunned.

"On what charge?" Jud asked.

"You're wanted for questioning in connection with the shooting of one Timothy Kelly."

Tim Kelly had been one of Mitchell's hands, murdered from ambush. "Why, that's impossible," Jud told the deputy. "I didn't shoot Tim Kelly. Tim and I were friends. Anyway, I was with Matt Taverner and some other fellows, looking for strays, the day that happened. There must be some mistake."

The deputy was apologetic. "That's possible, sir, mistakes happen all the time. But we still need to take you into Buffalo Notch."

"How long will I be there?"

"There's no telling. If we get this straightened out, you might be home as early as tonight."

Amy said, "Can't you ask your questions, or whatever it is you have to do, here?"

"No, ma'am, I'm sorry. It's a formality. There's papers to be filled out. There's other people to be questioned, too."

"Like who?" said Jud.

"I'm not at liberty to give out that information, sir."

Amy was getting angry. "But we have somewhere to go today."

The deputy looked down, scuffing his toe in the doorway. "It can't be helped, ma'am. I'm sorry."

The baby stuck his hand in Amy's face, but she pushed it aside. "I don't like this, Marshal. I don't like it at all."

Jud intervened, "It's all right, Amy. The deputy's just doing his job." To Thomas, he said, "I'll go with you."

The deputy looked relieved. "Thank you, sir. Your cooperation makes our job a whole lot easier."

"I'll get my clothes and a horse. You boys want some coffee?"

"We'd sure appreciate it, sir. There's a considerable chill out, and we been riding a good part of the night."

"There's biscuits, too. You're welcome to them."

Amy got fresh cups from the sideboard. The baby tried to pull them from her hand as she gave them out. After filling the cups from the coffeepot, she passed around the plate of biscuits.

"Thank you, ma'am," said Deputy Thomas. "Thanks, ma'am," said the other posse members as they ate and drank.

Amy felt ill at ease among these strangers. "Winter's coming," she observed, by way of conversation.

"Yes, ma'am, it sure is," said Deputy Thomas. "I hate to see it, too."

All this while, the Pratts' dog, a yellow hound, continued to sniff around and bark at the strange horses and riders.

At last Amy said, "Ulysses, stop! Ulysses! The way that dog carries on, you'd think you were red Indians."

Deputy Thomas smiled over his tin cup. "He's like us, ma'am—just doing his job. He don't know our smells. Come here, boy." He tried to get the dog to come to him, but the animal shied away.

Jud got his coat and hat and saddled a horse. "I don't know how long I'll be," he told Amy. "You go on to the Mitchells with Matt, when he comes."

"No," Amy said. "We'll wait till you get back."

"I'm telling you, there's no need to worry."

Amy was insistent. "We'll wait."

As Amy collected the coffee cups, Jud mounted his horse, along with the posse. "You ain't gonna put cuffs on me or nothin', are you?" he asked the deputy.

"No, sir. Nothing like that. Like I said, this is as much a formality as anything else." Deputy Thomas doffed his hat to Amy once more. "Thanks for the coffee, ma'am."

"You're welcome," Amy told him.

"I'll be back soon," Jud promised.

"All right." Amy waved tentatively, as Jud and the posse rode off in the direction of Buffalo Notch. The baby waved, too, following her example.

The little party rode for some miles. Jud engaged the deputies in small talk, mostly about the weather and horses. At last they approached a lone cottonwood, standing at the confluence of two small streams. A man was waiting there, on a horse.

As they drew closer, Jud saw that the man was small and dark complected, with a peaked leather cap and high-topped workman's boots. He held a coiled rope in one hand.

The posse reined in before the stranger. "This him?" said the small man. He spoke with some kind of foreign accent.

"Yeah," said Deputy Thomas.

"All right, let's get on with it."

Judson Pratt looked around, bewildered. Before he knew it, two of the posse members held pistols to his head. Dismounting, another grabbed his horse's bridle; still another bound his hands with a length of rope.

"What is this?" Jud demanded. "What's going on here?"

No one answered.

The small man handed Thomas something— a placard. "Stick this around his neck."

Thomas looped the placard over Jud's head. Jud was just able to read what it said: RUSTLER. It was signed: THE COMMITTEE OF TWENTY.

"Hey, wait, come on now," he said. "I ain't no rustler."

"Not no more, you ain't," cracked one of the posse members, and somebody laughed.

"Is this somebody's idea of a joke?" Jud cried.

"No joke," said the small man. He tossed the rope over a stout limb of the cottonwood tree. At the rope's end was a noose.

Jud went cold inside. His bowels loosened. "Come on, boys. Please, I swear to you, I never did no . . ."

He tried to get away, but two of the posse members now held his horse tight. "Goddamn it," he swore, "you can't do this. Not without a trial."

"You have had your trial," said the small man. "You are guilty."

"Deputy" Thomas drew Jud's horse forward and slipped the noose over Jud's neck. Jud fought him every inch of the way, yelling. "I got a wife and baby at home. What's going to happen to them?"

No one answered. Thomas tightened the noose behind Jud's right ear.

As the others drew back, the small man looked at Jud. "Do you have any last words to say?"

"You bet I do. You're a bunch of goddamn worthless . . ."

The small man smacked Jud's horse with his quirt. The horse shot out from underneath Jud, leaving its rider dangling from the tree limb.

Jud's neck didn't break in the fall. He choked to death, gagging, swinging and kicking in the air, the placard bouncing on his chest from his exertions.

He was still alive when the small man beckoned to the others. "Let's go."

The party of men rode off, leaving their victim to his fate.

CHAPTER 9

"'THE LORD SAYS, I WILL CONDEMN THE PERSON who turns away from me and puts his trust in man, in the strength of mortal man. He is like a bush in the desert, which grows in the dry wasteland . . .'"

Jack Mitchell droned on, reading from the Book of Jeremiah. Sam squirmed in his parlor chair. There was no church in the Basin, no pastor, no organized form of religion. Sunday service in the Mitchell house consisted of Bible reading and prayer. Lucy had read from the Book of Tobit, now it was Jack's turn.

In that respect, things hadn't changed much

since Sam was a boy here. He remembered how his Uncle Henry used to make him and Lucy read on Sundays, just like this. Uncle Henry's Bible had been the only book in the house. In the last years, those Sunday mornings had been about the only time Sam had seen his uncle sober.

Jack interrupted his thoughts. "Am I boring you, Sam?"

"Jack!" reprimanded Lucinda.

"No, I mean it," Jack said. "We're reading the Lord's Word here, and your cousin is daydreaming."

Sam looked sheepish. "I reckon my mind *was* somewhere else."

Lucinda sighed. She was not surprised. Her father had always come down on Sam for not paying attention during Sunday Bible reading.

Jack didn't share her perspective. "Living with Injuns the way you did, maybe you don't believe in the real God no more."

Sam ran his tongue around the inside of his mouth. "Seems to me there isn't much difference. God's God, no matter what you call him."

Jack's voice went up a notch. "You're not saying a heathen god is equal to the Almighty?"

"Apaches think we're the heathens," Sam pointed out.

"And what, exactly, do the Apaches call their 'God'?"

"Well, there's Ussen the Creator, and his son, Child of the Waters, who he fathered by the earthly virgin White Painted Woman, but there's other gods, too. They've got gods—or spirits—for just about anything you can think of."

Jack sneered contemptuously. "Child of the Waters, earthly virgins, White Painted Woman— surely you don't hold with such rubbish?"

"It makes about as much sense as what you're reading there."

Jack's jaw muscles worked. "From what I hear of their barbaric outrages, it seems to me your Apache friends could use a dose of the Good Book."

"It seems to me they'd be a lot better off if they were just left alone. Their system's fine for them; it beats me why anyone would want to change them."

"Because they're a lot of pagan . . . oh, never mind." Jack calmed his temper and continued reading.

Afterward they had breakfast. There was a platter of fried mountain trout that Jack had caught early that morning. Sam was content to help himself to flapjacks, bacon, and coffee. "Have some of the fish, Sam," urged Lucinda.

"Thanks, Lucy, but I don't eat fish anymore."

"Why not?"

Sam gave her a droll glance. He knew what kind of outburst his answer was going to provoke from Jack. "It's a habit I picked up from the Apaches."

Across the table, it sounded like Jack was strangling.

Lucy said, "Apaches don't eat fish?"

Sam shook his head. "They believe fish contain the spirits of evil women."

Jack banged his knife and fork on the table. "Your years with the Apaches seem to have left you more of an Indian than a white man."

Sam considered. "That's possible. I won't deny those years meant a lot to me."

"It's a wonder you don't go back to the Apaches, then," Jack said.

"If my Apache family hadn't been killed, I would never have left. There wouldn't be much for me to go back to, now."

"Who killed them?"

"White men," Sam said. "The army."

Jack looked smug. "Probably a damned good thing, too."

Lucy spoke up. "Jack, I'll thank you to be civil. Sam is family. He's our guest."

"Maybe he's your family. He ain't mine."

Lucy's blue eyes widened with anger. She rose from the table and left the room, going outside.

Sam and Jack were left alone at the table, staring at each other. If Jack hadn't been Lucy's husband, Sam would have been over the table and at his throat for that crack about his family, and he felt sure that Jack would have been happy to oblige him. At last Sam stood. "Good flapjacks," he remarked to Jack with a little smile. Then he went outside to join Lucinda.

He found her halfway to the stream, staring across it. He stood beside her.

Lucy looked up at him, and there were tears in her eyes. "I'm sorry for the way Jack's acted."

"It's all right. I've heard worse. I don't blame him, really. He's only saying what he knows."

"I just wish he knew a little more."

Sam put a comforting arm around her shoulder. "Dry those eyes. Folks will be coming soon for your meeting. You want to look pretty for them. You always were the prettiest girl in the Basin."

She sniffed. "That's because I was the only girl in the Basin."

"So you got some competition now. All the more reason to dry those eyes." With his free hand, he wiped away her tears. She smiled, and they hugged.

From the doorway of the ranch house Jack watched them, tight lipped.

CHAPTER 10

THE MEETING OF THE INDEPENDENT Cattleman's Association at the Pratt ranch would ordinarily have been an occasion for celebration, but Marty Singer's death had cast a pall over the affair.

The families began arriving late in the morning, by buckboard and on horseback. A few of the men wore Sunday suits, the rest had on clean versions of their everyday clothes. The women wore their best homespun dresses, or ones they had ordered from Eastern catalogues. Everyone contributed food, and soon the trestle tables set up outside the ranch house groaned with hams and chickens and venison, with pies of all descriptions, with bread and biscuits, and preserved fruits and jams. A steer turned on a spit nearby, crackling, its smell wafting over the area.

The children were unaffected by the Singer tragedy. They didn't see each other very much during the year, and now they yelled, played, and tussled with abandon.

The adults were different. They gathered in small groups around the food or the whiskey barrel, and their talk was of Marty Singer, and of the others who had died, and the consequences of it all.

"I've had it," said a rancher named Terry Ronan. "I got one of them warnings from the Committee of Twenty, just like Marty did, and I ain't stickin' around here waitin' for it to come true. Whoever sent it said to git, and I aim to git."

"You're pulling out?" said Tom Singer. Marty's younger brother was feeling better now.

"Leaving this week," Ronan allowed. "And I ain't taking no more than what I can fit in my wagon."

"What about the rest—your livestock, your gear?"

"They ain't worth my life and the lives of my family. Whoever wants them can have them, and welcome."

Another rancher, Miles Masterson, downed a glass of lemonade fortified with whiskey. "Why'n't you ask Clay Chandler to buy you out? No sense giving your land to Chandler for free if you can get him to pay for it. That's what I'm doing."

Jack Mitchell looked dismayed. "You're leaving, too, Miles?"

"Yep."

Ronan was unpersuaded by Masterson's argument. "No, I ain't waiting. And if you had any sense, you wouldn't wait, neither."

Lucinda had been listening to them. "You make it sound like we should all get out," she said.

Another man said, "Mebbe we should. What's the use in staying? I just found out one of Chandler's men filed a homestead claim on the headwaters of the creek that feeds my ranch. It's all phony, of course—he's doing it for Chandler. I hear he intends to dam the creek on his property."

"But that'll mean no water for you," said a big, bearded rancher named Mike Kennedy.

"I know," agreed the man helplessly.

"What are you going to do about it?" said a pudgy cowboy called Biscuit.

"What can I do? If I try to knock down the dam, they'll likely kill me."

Lucinda spoke up. "I'll tell you what you can do, what we can all do. We can fight."

"Fight how?" asked Sid Allison. He was an ex-cavalry sergeant who still wore his high-topped troop boots. "We can't prove anything against Chandler, and we can't match up with his hired artillery."

"That's right," said a man called Boyer. "I don't know nothing about killing. I just know cows and horses."

Lucinda said, "We have my cousin, Sam."

"What good can one man do?"

"Anyway," said another, "I don't know if I like having your cousin with us. Since he came, bodies are dropping quicker than ever."

"I agree," said Boyer. "I've always held myself a decent, God-fearing man. I don't hold much truck with bounty hunters."

Lucinda couldn't believe it. "You make Sam sound like some kind of criminal."

"He's a bounty hunter," said Sid Allison. "Two sides of the same coin."

Then Lucinda understood. "You've been talking to my husband." She looked at Jack, who turned away guiltily.

No one else spoke.

After a moment Jack cleared his throat. "Everybody seems to be here but Jud Pratt and his family. Matt Taverner's not here, either. Maybe they're waiting for him. Maybe their buckboard broke down. Whatever it is, let's go ahead and start the meeting."

Men gathered around or sat on overturned crates. Some of the more concerned women joined them, but many would not bother themselves with the men's business, no matter how important. In the background the children were still yelling and running around.

Jack began. "As you know, we've been warned by our friends at the Lazy H not to hold a roundup this fall. As many of you also know by now, I've called this meeting of the Association to discuss the possibility of holding a roundup before Chandler does."

There was lots of shifting around. Most of them had known this was coming, but things were different now that it was out in the open. There could be no more pretending, no more avoiding the consequences.

Tom Singer said, "We do that, and Chandler is going to think we're rustlers for certain."

"He's certain we're rustlers now," Jack replied, "so what's the difference? If we don't do it, we won't get any of this summer's calves. We won't have a trail herd to sell in Miles City this fall. By the time Chandler and his men are done combing the Basin, there won't be a steer worth a damn—sorry, ladies—that's not wearing the Lazy H."

Mike Kennedy said, "All right, say we go through with this. What happens to the steers and calves that Chandler could rightfully have expected to cull out for himself?"

Lucinda had a suggestion. "We'll do what we used to do. We'll pull out stock in proportion to the size of Clay's herd and let him have them. We'll play fair with him."

"Chandler has the biggest herd in the Basin," complained a lanky fellow named Pete Fleming. "If we do that, we'll spend a lot of our time out there working for him."

"That can't be helped, if we want to have a successful year," Lucinda said. "And we'll do it honestly—no running irons out there for changing brands."

Sid Allison said, "Who's going to take this cull to Chandler? That ain't a job I'd fancy."

"I'll do it," Sam said.

The men looked at him. He was different from them, with his high-topped Apache moccasins and the long scar that he wore like a badge of honor. Then they looked at each other. If he wanted the job, so be it. He had no standing among them. His fate did not concern them. It was a reaction Sam encountered all too many times before.

It grew dark; torches were lit. Several of the men produced fiddles and started playing. They began with mournful airs, to honor Marty Singer and their neighbors who were leaving the Basin, but their spirits couldn't be kept down for long. They started playing more spirited tunes, and men and women began dancing, to the accompaniment of hand clapping and whiskey-fueled shouts.

Sam saw Lucinda watching the dancers, tapping her feet to the music. Lucinda had always liked to dance—apparently she still did, despite her feelings toward men. Jack was nearby, with his whiskey glass, and Lucinda looked hopefully at him, but he pretended not to notice, and her face fell.

The fiddlers launched into "The Irish Washerwoman," to a new chorus of yells and foot stomping. Suddenly, Lucinda was at Sam's side. "Dance with me, Sam."

Sam hemmed and hawed and scraped the dirt with his foot.

"Please, Sam. You're the only one I had to dance with when we were young; you're the only one I have now. And I intend to make the most of it."

Sam said, "I don't think I . . ."

She stamped her foot. "Sam Slater, I order you to dance with me." It was the way she had gotten him to do things for her when they were children.

Sam let out his breath. "All right. Still the 'big sister,' aren't you?"

"Yes, I am."

As Jack Mitchell tossed back another drink and watched, Sam allowed himself to be led onto the patch of tamped-down earth that the guests were using as a dance floor. He put his arm around Lucy's waist, and they twirled in time to the music. This was the way they had both learned to dance. Lucy had employed Sam as an unwilling partner at sparsely attended social functions and over many a long winter's evening.

"You're doing fine," she told him above the music.

"I'm surprised," he replied. "I haven't danced since I left the Basin—not with a white woman, anyway."

"Did you dance with the Apache women?"

"A few. Of course their dancing's a bit different from this."

She gave him an arch look. "I'll make you tell me about it sometime."

He whirled her around when she wasn't expecting it, and she squealed with surprise and joy.

The fiddlers went from "The Irish Washerwoman" straight into "The Arkansas Traveler." Lucy and Sam kept time. Lucy's face was alight. The harsh frontier life—the backbreaking work, blazing summers, and frigid winters—had not destroyed her beauty. She looked even better, if anything. Her beauty seemed to regenerate itself from within, as if it were impervious to external assaults.

Then the music ended, and the sweating fiddlers paused for some refreshment. Lucy's face was flushed. "I haven't had that much fun in a long time. I can't get Jack to dance. He wouldn't even dance with me at our wedding—he's got no feel for it, and he's afraid of making a fool of himself in front of his friends."

A strand of her black hair had worked itself loose, and she brushed it away from her face. "Shall we dance again when the fiddlers come back?"

"It wouldn't do me any good to say no, would it?" Sam replied.

"It never did before."

"Then we'll dance."

"Let me get a glass of lemonade while we're waiting." Lucy headed toward the tables—she was too independent a woman to want a man to get it for her. One of the wives already there beckoned to her, and she stopped to talk.

While Sam was watching her, someone tapped his shoulder. He turned to see the lanky rancher named Pete Fleming. "Come on out back of the house for a minute," Fleming said. "Some of the boys need to talk to you."

Sam looked back at Lucy, who was still engaged by the women. "What about?" he asked Fleming.

"The situation here. What we're going to do about it."

Sam hesitated. "I told Lucy I'd—"

"It'll just take a minute. We'd sure appreciate it."

"All right then."

Sam and Fleming started away from the dancing. They rounded the corner of the ranch house, into the shadows between the house and the barn. The noise of the fiddlers and the dancers receded. There was a group of men waiting. It was hard to make them out in the dark.

Somebody grabbed Sam's arms from behind. Somebody else stepped out of the shadowy group and drove a fist into Sam's gut.

Sam doubled over, the breath knocked out of him. He was hit again. The blow was high this time and smashed into his chest, giving him a second to suck in needed air.

Another figure stepped forward. Sam swerved as best he could in the unseen man's grasp. The blow hit his ribs. Sam lashed up and out with his feet, kicking his assailant in the face, knocking him backward with a grunt of pain.

Sam gave a heave and threw the unseen man off his back. He turned and tried to run away, but his attackers tackled him and he went down in the dirt, fighting an unknown number of them, punching and kicking. Two of them got him by the arms this time, raising him up, just as somebody whistled a blow into his gut that almost knocked him out. His stomach rose into his throat. He dangled, helpless, in the grip of his assailants.

Now they really started in on him. Blow after blow, rhythmic, merciless, pounding his body to jelly. "Don't leave no marks on his face," said a voice from out of the fog of pain. "We don't want to upset Miss Lucinda."

Again and again they hit him, taking turns when they got tired. They hit him in his gut, his ribs, his chest. He was sick all over himself and still they hammered away. Everything was spinning. His mouth was full of blood and vomit. Snot ran from his nose. His legs had lost all strength; he was being kept upright only by the men who held him.

At last it stopped. A voice—it might have been Fleming's—said, "Get out of the Basin, Slater. We don't want you around here."

"You ain't our kind," said another voice.

"You ain't nobody's kind," added a third.

This was followed by a tremendous kick to Sam's groin, so powerful that it seemed to lift his scrotum out through the top of his head. He gagged and retched with pain.

Then whoever was holding him let him go, and he dropped to the ground. He lay there, moaning, his mouth in the dirt, listening to receding footsteps as his attackers returned to the gathering. He heard low laughter.

Sam curled up in a ball of pain. He was afraid to move, afraid to make the pain worse. His insides felt like they were busted to pieces. On the other side of the ranch house there was music and laughter, children calling. On this side Sam lay moaning in his own vomit.

He began snaking back and forth, and each movement brought pain so intense that sweat poured out of him. He almost blacked out, but he bit his lip and kept going, fighting through the pain. At last he managed to bring himself to his hands and knees. He remained that way awhile, until the world stopped spinning. Then he crawled toward a nearby wagon. He reached out, grabbed a wheel, and hauled himself slowly to his feet.

The blood rushed from his head, and he almost passed out. He steadied himself and waited till his breathing had returned to something like normal. He pushed away from the wagon and stood without support. His legs were wobbly, and he staggered a bit before getting his balance.

Slowly, a step at a time, gritting his teeth against the pain, he walked back to the gathering. He turned the corner of the house, into the light. People stopped what they were doing and stared at him, covered with dirt and vomit, his shirt ripped to shreds.

Lucinda ran up and took his arm. "Sam, what happened?"

He shook her off and kept going.

He found Jack Mitchell and his friends by the whiskey. Jack hadn't been one of the men behind the house, but Sam knew who had put them up to it. The men were talking and laughing, but they stopped when they saw Sam coming.

He halted in front of Jack, staring him dead in the eye. He said, "Get this straight, Mitchell. I don't give a damn about you or any of your friends, but Lucy is my only kin in this world. I'm going to help her keep this ranch if I have to kill every one of you to do it."

Jack set down his glass and stepped away from the rest of the men. "Maybe we should start now."

Sam started forward. "That's fine with me. . . ."

Both men raised their fists. They were stopped by a commotion from the direction of the creek—it sounded like a buckboard, coming hard.

There was splashing as the buckboard crossed the creek. People gathered around. "It's Amy Pratt," someone said, "and Matt Taverner."

Taverner reined in the team and braked the wagon. Beside him on the seat, Amy held her young son. She looked desperate and worried.

"What's wrong?" Lucinda asked, climbing up beside Amy, putting an arm around her.

"Where's Jud at?" added somebody else.

"He's been arrested," Amy said. She was almost beside herself. "A deputy marshal from Helena took him to Buffalo Notch for questioning about Tim Kelly's murder."

"Kelly!" said Lucinda. "Jud didn't have anything to do with that."

"I know. They left early this morning. Matt and me waited for Jud to come back, but he didn't, and now I'm awful worried. I'm afraid something's happened to him."

CHAPTER 11

THE ASSEMBLED CATTLEMEN AND THEIR families looked at one another. Jack Mitchell said, "Ladies, if you'd be so kind, you'd best start brewing up some coffee. I'll take half the men into Buffalo Notch and see what's happened to Jud. Kennedy, you stay here with the rest. Watch over the women and children. I don't know what's going on, but I don't like it."

"What about weapons?" somebody asked.

"We have a few extra lying around here. I expect some of you brought your own. We'll have to make do with that. Lucinda, will you take care of Amy and her child?"

Lucinda nodded, as she helped the terrified Mrs. Pratt from the buckboard.

Pots of coffee were boiled, and the men gulped them down, trying to sober up from all the whiskey they'd drunk. "Those who brought horses take them," Jack said. "The rest of you can borrow some of my stock."

Horses were roped and saddled. Weapons were checked. Tom Singer was one of those who wanted to go. Jack looked at him sharply. "You in shape to ride, Tom? Two days ago you were too weak to sit in bed, much less on a horse."

"It was just the ague," Tom explained. "It goes away quick. I can keep up."

Jack wasn't so sure, but he said, "All right."

In the rush and confusion, Sam and his confrontation with Jack were forgotten. The cattlemen assumed Sam had gotten their message. He leaned against one of the food tables, steadying himself. His insides were so busted up, it hurt to breathe.

Lucinda left Amy and her child for a moment and came over to him. "Aren't you going with them?"

Sam shook his head. "I'm not wanted. They made that pretty clear."

"They could use you if there's trouble."

"If there's trouble, I'll be there. But I'll do it my way."

The children, except for the eldest, were put

to bed. The women gathered around Amy Pratt, comforting her and talking among themselves in low, worried tones, while the men who were staying at the ranch set up a guard. Jack and his half of the men mounted their horses and started for the Pratt place.

It was another frosty night, and the party hunkered down as they rode. Some had rifles, some pistols; only a few carried both. They picked up the posse's trail at the Pratt ranch and followed it toward town. It was just past dawn when they came in sight of the lone cottonwood at the confluence of the two streams. Even at this distance they knew whose body was dangling from one of the tree's limbs.

"Aw, shit," swore one of the men in disgust.

They rode on in. Judson Pratt's youthfully bearded face had turned black. The birds had already been at work on him.

"'Rustler,'" said Jack, reading the placard that hung from the dead man's neck. "Jud was no more a rustler than he had anything to do with Tim Kelly's death."

Tom Singer said, "Yeah, and I'll bet the fellows who took him away weren't deputy marshals, neither."

"The Committee of Twenty," said the rancher named Boyer. "Who are they?"

"Who do you think?" replied Jack bitterly. "Clay Chandler's men." He went on. "We better cut him down. We'll put him on one of the horses and take him to my place. Amy can take him home from there. Phil, you and Biscuit can ride double, can't you?"

The red-haired cowboy called Phil nodded. As Jack and a group of the men cut the rope and lowered Jud's body, Sid Allison said, "I ain't lookin' forward to another funeral."

The lanky cattleman named Pete Fleming sat his horse next to Jack's. "We going after the fellows who did this?" he asked.

"What good would it do?" Jack said. "Even if we caught them, what chance would we have against them? Half of us aren't properly armed, and now we've got two men riding double. I don't fancy taking on Chandler's gunmen at that kind of disadvantage."

With difficulty Jack and the others hoisted Jud Pratt's stiffening body across Phil's horse. Jack bound the dead man's hands and feet together so that he would not fall off. When the job was done, Tom Singer blew on his chilled hands to warm them. Tom was holding up a lot better than Jack had expected. He said, "Jack, maybe we should reconsider this early roundup idea of yours."

"Yeah," agreed Boyer. "We go through with that, and we're all going to end up like Jud here."

"That would mean a whole year without income," Jack pointed out. "And what about all the calves out there, the unbranded yearlings? Do you want Chandler to get them?"

"We'd still have our land," argued Tom. "We'd still have our lives."

"For how long? It's only a matter of time before Chandler comes for you, just like he did for Jud, and your brother Marty, and all the others."

Boyer said, "Well, if that's true what's the good in having a roundup, or even in staying here? Why don't we all just pack up and go, like Miles Masterson and Ronan?"

"What's wrong?" Jack asked him. "You scared?"

"Damn right I am," Boyer replied.

Jack calmed down. "All right, I'm scared, too. But I'm not going to quit, and neither will my wife. I'm telling you, if we stick together, we . . ."

"We *been* sticking together, and Chandler is killing us off one by one."

"We can fort up together," Jack said. "The whole Basin, just like they did in Texas during the war. Till this blows over."

The ex-soldier Sid Allison said, "Hell, Jack, that could take years. In the meantime Chandler is free to burn our homes and steal our herds."

"We can rebuild. At least this way Chandler couldn't get at us personally."

The ranchers looked doubtful.

"All right," Jack said at last, "so maybe it's a dumb idea. But do any of you have a better one?"

"Not short of killing Chandler," said Fleming.

"That'd be murder," Jack told him. "We can't do that."

Fleming said, "We could form a Committee of Vigilance, just like this so-called Committee of Twenty. God knows we got cause."

"How would we do it? Chandler's protected by a couple dozen gunmen—not to mention his other hands. We'd never get close to him."

Somebody said, "What about that bounty hunter cousin of Lucinda's? Maybe he'd do it for us."

"Slater?" sneered Jack. "He's no use. Anyway I doubt he'll even be around when we get back—not after what you boys did to him."

A couple of the men chuckled.

Jack went on. "No, our only choice is to stay the course and trust that better times are ahead."

Boyer spoke for the group. "I'll tell you what, Jack. I don't want to give up, but I don't feel like dying young, neither. We can stay in this a little while longer, but there's a limit to what we're prepared to take."

"I'm staying in till they kill me," Jack said defiantly.

"I know," said Boyer. "That's what's got us worried."

Jack said, "In the meantime, we'd best plan to go into Buffalo Notch as a group when we buy supplies for the roundup. It'll be safer that way."

The sun was just coming up, bringing welcome warmth, as the little party of cattlemen remounted and started back toward the Mitchell place with its sad burden. When they had disappeared over the horizon, another figure approached the cottonwood tree from the east. Sam Slater had followed the cattlemen at a distance, close enough to be of use if there was trouble, far enough back that they wouldn't suspect his presence. He had watched them take the body from the cottonwood's limb. Now he rode closer.

He dismounted near the tree and let his horse drink from the stream and graze on the surrounding grass. He looked at the discarded placard, then tossed it away. The cattlemen had stirred up the ground near the tree, so he had to go a ways to pick up the tracks of Jud Pratt's killers.

There had been six of them. Only three had dismounted during the encounter, all wearing high-heeled cowboy boots. Sam didn't find the prints of the small man with the square-toed work boots, but that didn't mean the small man hadn't been there. Sam noted that one of the killers' horses had a v-shaped nick in the shoe of its near foreleg.

Sam remounted, following the tracks. It hurt to ride, from the beating he had gotten last night, but he suffered through the pain, the way he had been taught by the Apaches. He expected the killers to head for either Buffalo Notch or the Lazy H Ranch, or to split themselves between the two.

Sam did not want to go to town, because by now Marshal Cummings—as well as everyone else—would have learned about the reward on his head and be looking to gun him down. But the Lazy H was a big spread. If the killers had gone there, he might get lucky and catch up to them if they stopped for breakfast or a rest.

The sun rose higher. The vapor disappeared from Sam's breath, and the chill eased out of his battered bones. It was another fine day, but thick clouds building to the northwest told of bad weather to come. Might even be snow before it was done, he thought. He had to laugh at that. Back in Tucson it was still a hundred in the shade.

The killers had left the stream and climbed into a nearby range of hills. They had then reversed their direction, winding among the rugged hills to throw off pursuit. They had ridden over rocky ledges and for a good mile along a creek bed, but Sam managed to stay with them. A freshly broken twig here; an overturned rock, its damp side to the sun, there; the scrape of a horseshoe on shale—all these were indicators. The killers might have lost a lot of pursuers, but to a man trained by Apaches it was like following the Overland Trail. Sam kept his rifle ready as he rode. These hills were heavily wooded and jumbled with boulders—ambush country, if that was what the killers had in mind.

Then the tracks reversed direction once more. They left the hills and headed down into the valley of the Arrowhead. The killers made no more attempt to hide their trail, but followed the river in a generally northwest direction, toward the building clouds. A chill wind was blowing, and Sam drew his coat closer around him, turning up the collar.

The tracks crossed the Arrowhead at a ford and headed across the open range. Sam passed a small group of longhorns grazing, eyeing him warily. He jogged his mount closer to them, and before they turned away he was able to make out their brand—the Lazy H. He was on Chandler's range. He looked around. He had once known this country well, but it had been empty then. There had been no white men this side of the Arrowhead.

He paused to think. Should he go on? He had found out what he had come to learn—Jud Pratt's killers had been working for Chandler. There was still a possibility he could come upon them unawares, but he had to balance that with the thought that Chandler could now catch him just as easily.

His dilemma was suddenly settled for him, as he saw riders cresting a distant swell. There were five of them. They saw Sam at the same time and turned his way. They could only be Chandler's men, and Sam knew they were not likely to treat strangers gently. He turned his horse and started back for the Arrowhead.

The riders came after him, riding hard now. Sam had no way of telling if they were Jud Pratt's killers, but he bet they weren't, because their horses looked fresh. Sam's own horse was worn down from a night of riding and a day of climbing the hills, and that was going to be a very big problem. Sam thought about stopping to fight, one man against five, but that was long odds here on the open range without the advantage of surprise, and anyway he couldn't be sure there weren't more of Chandler's men right behind. Sam's horse didn't have enough left in him for a long chase, though, and unless these cowhands gave up, Sam was going to be forced to fight them.

He kept his horse at a controlled gallop, trying to hold something back for a last spurt. Behind him, the riders drew closer. He heard them yelling to one another. He saw rifles and pistols in their hands.

If he could cross the Arrowhead, they might give up and leave him alone. It was a slim hope. They had an angle on him, and even if he got across the river, he had an idea they would keep going till they had run him down. A bullet whined past him. He heard the flat report of a rifle. Someone had tried a ranging shot. He hadn't missed by much, either, even at a gallop—

that was good shooting. These were no thirty-dollar-a-month waddies then; they were Chandler's hired guns. Sam swore to himself and forgot about the river. He would have to fight.

There was a long hill off to his left, with patches of pine woods running down it like ragged carpet. Those woods were as good a place to fort up as he was going to find, and he guided his horse toward them. Another bullet hummed past him.

Sam kicked his horse into a flat-out gallop, but the beast had nothing left to give. It began slowing noticeably, its neck and flanks lathered with sweat. Behind him, Chandler's men were almost within pistol range. With a sinking heart, Sam knew that he was not going to make the woods. He would have to fight Chandler's gunmen in the open, and against experienced men that was a five-dollar phrase for committing suicide. Still, he had no choice.

He drew in his breath, preparing to haul in on the horse's reins, then shoot the animal and use it for cover, when he saw a puff of smoke from the woods ahead of him. Had he been caught in a crossfire? No, the bullet was aimed at his pursuers. Behind Sam, one of Chandler's men grabbed his shoulder and almost fell from the saddle, while a comrade reached over and grabbed the wounded man's bridle, steadying his horse. Another shot, and one of the gunmen's charging horses stumbled, then fell on its side. The rider scrambled clear. He swung up behind one of his friends, and the group of them retreated from their unknown assailant, followed by two more shots.

Sam's horse was all in, breathing heavily. Sam wasn't in much better shape himself. His stomach and ribs throbbed from last night's beating. He dismounted, easing his saddle cinches and resting a minute. Then he walked his horse toward the stand of pines. As he drew close, his rescuer rose from behind a fallen log.

"Lucy!" said Sam, stopping in surprise.

His cousin grinned, showing white teeth. Her wide-brimmed hat hung behind her on its chin strap. "I thought you might need some help," she said.

"You followed me all the way from your ranch. I never guessed."

Lucinda laughed. "Remember how we used to play Indians? I was always able to sneak up on you without you knowing." She stuffed fresh shells into the breech of her rifle, keeping an eye on the horizon. "I don't know what I would have done if you hadn't headed for this woods. I came here as soon as I saw you in trouble. I'm surprised you didn't see me."

"I must have just missed you," Sam said. He drew up to her and hugged her. "I've got to thank you, big sister. You saved my bacon."

She regarded him with a steady eye. "I recall you doing the same for me."

"Jack's going to be angry when he finds out where you've gone."

"He'll just have to be angry then, won't he?"

"I think he'd have been just as happy if Chandler's boys had finished me off."

"Oh, Sam. He's not that bad. Really, if you knew him like I do, you'd . . ."

"I know. I'd like him." Sam looked behind them. There was no sign of the five riders. "We better get going. They've likely gone for reinforcements."

Lucinda grew serious. "At least now there's no doubt about who had Jud Pratt killed."

"Be hard to prove, though. Killers like that, they probably come into the Basin, do the job, get their pay, and get out. Chandler can always hire more for the next job."

"Sam, I'm scared. What can we do? How are we going to stop Clay?"

Sam let out his breath. "I been thinking maybe I'll pay him a visit, see if he'll listen to reason."

"How will you get to him? There's a reward on your head. His men will shoot you on sight."

Sam looked to the darkening northeast sky. He could smell rain in the air. Then he smiled. "First they've got to see me."

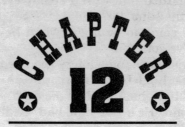

CHAPTER 12

IT WAS RAINING BY THE TIME JACK MITCHELL and his party returned to the ranch. All of those who had been left behind gathered to see them come in, crowding under the shelter of the ranch house porch, spilling onto the open ground outside. The anxious watchers knew that something was wrong when they saw two men riding double. Then they saw the blanket-wrapped figure slung over Phil's horse.

Amy Pratt's hand flew to her mouth. "Oh, God," she cried. "Oh, God."

Some of the women comforted her. "Be strong, Amy. Maybe it's not Jud." Other women anxiously scanned the returning riders, trying to determine if their own men were safe. By the time the party splashed across the stream, individuals could be identified and accounted for, and everyone knew that the dead man was indeed Judson Pratt.

The riders halted in front of the ranch house. Rain dripped from their hats and sodden coats. The temperature had been falling all afternoon, and they were chilled to the bone. Amy Pratt was nearly hysterical now. "Let me take your baby," said Mrs. Boyer, trying to lift Jud Junior from her arms.

"No," she cried, pulling away, holding onto the child with grim determination.

Two of the women gently took her arms. "Come inside the house, then. You'd better sit down."

But she shook them off and stepped from the porch into the mud, approaching Jack as he dismounted. "What happened to Jud?"

Jack looked into her face, where tears mingled with the rain. He took her shoulders. "Look, Amy, maybe it's best if . . ."

"I want to know!" she demanded. "I have a right to know! He was my husband!"

Jack hesitated. He looked at the others—men, women, children—who had gathered around. He spoke in a defeated voice. "He was hung. Lynched. Whoever . . . whoever did it left a note claiming he was a rustler."

There were murmurs and cries of outrage from the crowd. Amy couldn't believe it. "But Jud never . . ."

"I know, I know," Jack told her, smoothing her wet hair with his hand.

"It's Clay Chandler, isn't it? He did this."

Jack nodded. "Most likely."

Turning away from Jack, Amy lifted the blanket from her dead husband's head before anyone could stop her. She looked at his swollen, blackened face, pecked by birds, with the rope burns around his neck.

"Oh, my poor Jud."

Her knees went weak and she swooned. Jack caught her and the baby at the same time, holding onto them awkwardly until some of the women took them from him. "Get her in the house," he told the women. "Put a blanket over her and give her some brandy."

The ladies took Amy and her baby inside, while the children wandered off to talk about what they had just seen. The rest of Jack's party dismounted and led their tired horses toward the barn, heads bowed against the rain. Jack looked around. "Where's Lucinda?" he asked Mike Kennedy.

The bearded Kennedy, who had been left in charge while Jack was gone, said, "She's gone. Left right after you did."

Anger flared in Jack's tired face. "What about Slater?"

"He's gone, too."

Jack would have sworn, but he didn't want the others to see how mad he was. "Let's go up on the gallery," Kennedy suggested, "and get out of this rain."

Jack and Kennedy, along with the men who had stayed behind, stepped onto the ranch house porch. They were joined by the rest of Jack's party, coming back from the barn. Somebody produced a bottle of whiskey, and the wet, shivering men passed it around.

Jack took the bottle with trembling fingers. A drink of the fiery liquid eased his shaking. He took another, then sighed with relief. He'd needed that. Kennedy said, "Are you sure Chandler's men killed Jud?"

"Sure as we can be," Jack said. "Don't know who else would have done it—or why."

Matt Taverner, Jud Pratt's friend and some-time employee, said, "We better be getting back to our homes, Jack. We got our property to look after, and our stock."

Jack nodded wearily. "All right, but be careful."

Young Tom Singer, who seemed to have fully recovered from his bout with the ague, said, "What about Buffalo Notch? When do we go in for supplies?"

Jack thought for a second. "Day after tomorrow. We want to get started on the roundup as soon as we can, before Chandler can stop us.

The boys from the upper end of the Basin can meet here. We'll ride south and pick up the rest of you at Boyer's place—he's closest to town."

The other men agreed. Jack added, "Don't let word of this get out. We don't want trouble while we're in town —and we don't want Chandler raiding our ranches while we're gone. Make sure your hands and families keep close to home that day."

The men nodded. "All right."

"That's settled, then," Jack said. "Come on, let's go inside and get dry."

Over the course of the afternoon, the families departed to their homes. Matt Taverner drove Amy and Jud Junior, with Jud Senior's body under a tarp in the back of the buckboard. At last Jack was left by himself. Outside, the empty trestle tables gleamed in the cold rain. The barbeque spit looked forlorn. The women had done a lot of cleaning up, but there was still work to be done. Inside, Jack pulled the whiskey jug from its hiding place in the chair and began to drink. When the jug was empty, Jack opened another. The dogs lay before the fire, sleeping.

Toward evening the dogs came alert. The clopping of hoofs told Jack that Lucinda was back. He pushed himself from the chair and went onto the gallery, leaning against the awning post for support. His reddish brows beetled together as he watched his wife ride slowly toward the house in the rain.

Jack held the bridle of Lucinda's horse, Honeysuckle, as she dismounted. He could barely conceal his anger. "Where have you been?"

Lucinda didn't answer. She was cold and wet and tired, and she didn't want to argue. She led Honeysuckle toward the barn, and Jack followed her. "You've been with your Indian friend, haven't you?"

Lucinda rounded on him. "Sam is not a friend, he's my cousin. And he's not an Indian, he's as white as you are. And even if he was an Indian, what difference would it make?"

"To you, none, apparently."

"That's right," she told him. "Sam wants to help us."

"Not 'us,'" Jack corrected. "'You.'"

"It's the same thing."

"Not to me, it isn't. Not when you take every opportunity to go off alone with him."

A warning note crept into Lucinda's voice. "Jack, don't start this again."

"I'll start what I please. Your so-called cousin hasn't come back to help us, he's come to renew an old romance."

Lucinda reached out and slapped Jack's face, hard. Jack flared and started forward, but managed to restrain himself. Lucinda looked at him with disdain. "If you want to help us, why don't you sober up?"

Jack glared at her, and she turned away.

"Don't wait up for me," she said. "I'm sleeping in the barn tonight."

She started walking away with Honeysuckle. Jack called after her. "And Slater, where is he?"

"None of your business."

Jack watched her go. Then he went back into the house and started drinking again. He drank himself unconscious and slept the night in the chair.

When he woke it was well after dawn. He was stiff and cold. His head throbbed, and it felt like a huge buffalo tongue had been stuffed into his mouth in place of his own. He stood with a start, realizing where he was. Breakfast should have been ready, but the stove was cold and Lucinda was nowhere to be seen. He stumbled into the bedroom, but Lucinda was not there. Then he remembered the fight they'd had and how she had sworn to sleep in the barn.

Scrunching eyes against the pain, he lurched outside. He said such stupid things when he was drinking. He would have to make it up to her somehow. Dimly—because not only was he hungover, he was still drunk—he realized there was snow on the ground as he made his way to the barn. He searched inside but Lucinda was not there, nor was her horse Honeysuckle.

She had gone again, to be with Slater.

CHAPTER 13

THE COLD RAIN SLANTED DOWN, DRUMMING on the roofs of the Lazy H Ranch. The Lazy H was a sprawling establishment, with sheds and barns and corrals. It was informal and easy-going, the kind of place where a woman's influence had never been felt. The biggest building was the bunkhouse. Though it had been constructed for a large number of men, it was still crowded, not only with regular cowhands, but with those who had been hired solely for their abilities with a gun.

Clay Chandler took his meals in the bunkhouse with his men. He considered himself one of them. He worked side by side with them on the ranch, never asking them to do anything—from branding calves, to chopping firewood, to breaking horses—that he wouldn't do himself. He put on no airs. He dressed like the men and worked like them, and the men respected him for it.

Right now supper was over, and the men took their tin plates back to the cookhouse. Afterward they lounged around—joking, playing cards, or mending gear. Clay sat at one of the tables, paying off Harold Thomas and the crew of men who had been involved in the hanging of Jud Pratt. Nearby, but apart from the others, sat a dark, smallish man wearing a leather coat and peaked leather workman's cap. The regular hands went out of their way to pretend that they didn't notice what was going on.

Chandler counted out a stack of greenbacks and slid it across the table. "Two hundred. There you are."

One of Thomas's men took the stack and pocketed it. "Thanks, Mister Chandler."

Chandler said, "You boys know what to do now?"

Thomas, who had once actually served as a Deputy U.S. Marshal before succumbing to the lure of easy money, replied, "Right. We'll be pulling out in the morning."

"Swimming, if this rain don't stop," cracked one of the men.

Chandler took a stubby pencil and a pad of paper from the pocket of his checked flannel shirt. He scribbled something on a sheet of the paper, tore it off, and handed it to Thomas. "This is the man you'll deliver the cattle to in Bannack. You'll be paid for them there."

Thomas read the name and folded the paper, slipping it into his own pocket.

Chandler went on. "Don't try to cheat me, to sell those cattle for yourselves and keep the money. I have a long reach."

Thomas grinned. "We know you do. Besides, we might want to come back here and work for you again some day."

One of the other 'deputies' agreed. "Yeah, I ain't never got paid so good for havin' fun."

Chandler nodded in dismissal. Thomas and his men moved away, slapping each other's backs in congratulations. They would have liked a drink, but Chandler didn't allow liquor in the bunkhouse.

Chandler turned to the small, dark man in the leather cap. "You did another good job."

"That is what you pay me for," replied the man in his accented voice.

"I'm informed that Mitchell and his bunch are going into Buffalo Notch the day after tomorrow, to get supplies for their roundup."

"Is that so?" said the small man. "Perhaps I should be there to greet them."

"Perhaps you should."

"What about Slater?" the small man added.

"I hear he's out of the picture. Apparently Mitchell and his friends don't want a man with Slater's reputation helping them."

"Then Mitchell and his friends are even more stupid than I thought. It's a pity. I would like to have collected that two-thousand-dollar reward on Slater."

"You still can," Chandler told him. "If Slater's around when this is over, you're welcome to him."

The small man smiled and nodded thanks. Chandler went on. "There will also be a bonus for you when the last member of the 'Independent Cattlemen's Association,' or whatever they call themselves, leaves the Basin— dead or alive."

The small man liked that. "I enjoy working for you, Mister Chandler. Truly I do."

"Thank you. I try to keep my employees satisfied. Now, if you'll excuse me?"

Chandler rose, buttoning his coat, and left the bunkhouse. Flakes of snow were mixed with the rain now. The cold seeped through his boots as he squished across the waterlogged ground to his house.

Sleeping by himself was the only thing that set Chandler apart from his men. His house was a two-room affair of logs and sod. He could have built a larger place—with his money he could have built a mansion—but he had grown up without creature comforts, and he didn't need any more than he had now. He would build the mansion when he had Lucinda.

He missed a step, splashing in an icy puddle, and he swore. Lucinda did that to him; she always had. Just the thought of her set his hands itching, and he thought about her day and night. It had been that way since the first time he'd seen her. He'd never loved a woman the way he loved Lucinda. She had a combination of beauty and spirit that excited him. Possessing her would be like possessing a prize race horse. And when Jack Mitchell was dead, Clay was going to possess her.

Clay had been born in Tennessee. When he was young his family had moved to Texas, for free land. Life in Texas had been a constant struggle—against the weather, against Indians, against swarms of insects that stripped the crops bare in the fields. Food had been corn dodgers and whatever his pa and older brothers could hunt. As soon as he'd been old enough, Clay had joined a cattle drive to Kansas. His wages from that drive had bought him the first new clothes he'd ever worn. Clay had decided to become a rancher, but the best range land in Texas was being grabbed off by the big spreads. Then Clay had heard about the opportunities and unclaimed lands to be had in Montana. Saving his money from several trail drives, he'd purchased a small herd and taken it north. He had brought one of the first longhorn herds into this territory; before that, most of the cattle here were eastern shorthorns.

Clay had always been ambitious, but his ambition had not begun to consume him until Lucinda Slater—that had been her name then—had turned down his proposal of marriage. Clay had believed that she refused him because she didn't think he was good enough for her, and he had sworn then and there that he would become good enough for any woman. He had sworn to build an empire, to own land as far as the eye could see. He had sworn to put himself in a position where Lucinda could not refuse him again—no matter how much work it took or how many people he had to trample to achieve his goals.

And now he was so close to those goals that he could almost taste it. He was ready to savor his moment of victory.

He reached his house. He shook the rain off his coat and stepped in. There was no fire burning, and the house was cold and damp. Clay lit a kerosene lamp by the door. He trimmed the wick, turned, and almost jumped out of his skin because there was a man sitting in his chair with a pistol pointed at him.

"Slater!" he breathed.

"Evening, Chandler," replied Sam.

Chandler's heart raced in shock. "How—how did you get in here? How did you get past my men, my dogs?"

Sam smiled. "It's not hard, if you know how."

"What are you, some kind of Indian or something?"

"Something like that."

Chandler thought about all the men in the bunkhouse, so close . . .

"Don't get any ideas about calling for help," Sam told him. "You'll be dead before the first words are out of your mouth. And with this rain, your men might not even hear the pistol shot."

Chandler felt trapped and angry. "All right, you're here. What do you want?"

"I want you to call off your Committee of Twenty."

"I don't know what you're talking about."

"I think you do. I want the small ranchers left alone."

"Or what?" Chandler said.

"Or I'll kill you."

Chandler said, "They call that murder, you know."

"I'm already wanted for one murder. Another won't make any difference."

"Why don't you just kill me now?"

"I thought about it," Sam confessed. "But I never killed a man without giving him a chance first."

"That's very noble of you."

"Just trying to be fair."

Chandler rubbed his stubbled chin. "So what am I supposed to do—let these rustlers keep stealing my cattle?"

"They're not rustlers, Chandler. You know that as well as I do."

"Really? Then who's been raiding my herd?"

Sam hesitated. Chandler sounded sincere. "I don't know. You sure somebody *is* stealing from you?"

"I'm sure. We find the tracks on our range all the time, plus our count at roundups is always less than we expect. How else do you explain the other herds in the Basin getting so big so fast?"

"They're losing cattle, too."

Chandler snorted. "Is that what your friend Mitchell tells you?"

Sam smiled, still sore from the pounding he'd received last night. "Jack Mitchell isn't exactly my friend."

"How much is he paying you? I can offer more."

"I'm doing this for personal reasons."

"Ah, yes, the prodigal cousin. I remember now—you and Lucinda are related, aren't you? And the man you murdered, wasn't he . . . ?"

Sam rose from the chair. "I didn't come here to make small talk, Chandler. You've had one warning. There won't be another."

Suddenly Chandler felt like he had the upper hand. "All right, Slater, you've said your piece. Now, how do you intend to get out of here? The moment you're through that door, I'll have thirty men after you, and with that reward on your head, they won't need much incentive."

"It's easy," Sam told him. He pushed forward the chair, which was cleverly constructed from cattle horns, with a rawhide seat and back. "Have a seat."

Chandler hesitated.

"I said sit, or I'll wrap this pistol barrel around your skull."

He meant it. Chandler swallowed and did as he had been told. Sam took a length of rope and bound the cattleman's hands behind the chair, then he unknotted Chandler's bandanna and tied it around his mouth as a gag. With another length of rope he fastened Chandler's ankles. "Your boys'll find you in the morning."

Chandler struggled in the chair, mumbling threats through the gag.

Admiring his handiwork, Sam smiled and holstered his pistol. "Good night, Mister Chandler. Pleasant dreams."

Then he was out the door, into the rain.

CHAPTER 14

WHEN THE STORM ENDED, THERE WAS ABOUT an inch of snow on the ground. The clouds blew away early the next morning, and the sun came out, and except in patches of shade, the snow had melted by the time Sam reached his destination.

He and Lucinda had gone there often as children. It was an old trapper's cabin, situated near one of the streams that ran out of Lake McKenzie. Sam and Lucinda had never known who the trapper was—he had departed long before they arrived in the Basin—but the ruins of his cabin had still been there, along with some badly rusted and pitted beaver traps. They had never known why he'd left, either. Had the beaver been trapped out? If so, why hadn't he taken his traps with him? Had he been killed by Indians? By disease? By a bear? They had never known, and they never would—maybe that had been part of their fascination with the place.

If the beaver had been trapped out, they were back now; their conical lodges rising from the stream gave proof of that. The water rang with the slapping of their tails. A broad meadow ran down to the stream, where the rushes stood golden in the autumn sunshine. The cabin site was set back a ways, near a grove of sycamores.

Lucinda was waiting for Sam where the cabin had been. She had brought him a fresh horse, as he had requested, along with a dry saddle blanket, some food, and a change of clothing. In the shade behind her, snow still coated the red-gold leaves of the sycamores, and tufts of grass poked through its white carpet in the hollows. Despite the sun it was cold, and Lucinda stamped her booted feet to warm them as Sam rode up.

"I was worried about you," she said. "I was afraid Clay's men might have killed you."

"Your husband's friends already made a start on that," Sam remarked. His ribs and gut still hurt from the beating, and a night in the saddle hadn't made them feel any better.

"I'm sorry about that, Sam. I . . ."

"It wasn't your fault," Sam said as he dismounted.

"But Jack. I blame myself. I never thought . . ."

"Forget it." Sam looked around. All that remained of the cabin now was the crumbled stone fireplace, along with the slowly decaying beaver traps. Brush and saplings hid all other traces of human habitation. "Not much left of it, is there?" Sam said.

"No," Lucinda replied, "and what's still here will be gone before long. This used to be our secret place."

They paused, remembering picnics and berry fights they'd had here, times they'd sheltered from the rain in the old cabin. Then she said, "I still don't see why you had me meet you here, instead of coming back to the ranch."

"I think it's best I keep away from the ranch," Sam told her. "It's pretty well known that I've got a reward on my head, and I don't want to be tempting your friends. Plus, it could be embarrassing to you if that U.S. Marshal from Helena shows up. Jack doesn't want me there anyway. What did he say when you came home yesterday?"

"Don't ask," Lucinda said. "When I left this morning he was passed out in his chair, with his whiskey jug beside him. He and the boys are going into Buffalo Notch tomorrow, to buy supplies for the roundup."

Lucinda had built a small fire and brewed coffee, and Sam knelt and poured himself a cup. "You always were thoughtful," he told her.

"I figured you'd be cold. How'd you make out with Clay?"

Sam rose again, spreading his hands. "Chandler is either telling the truth or he's a good liar. He swears his cattle are being rustled. He thinks your husband and his friends are doing it."

"You don't believe him, do you?"

"I don't know." Sam drank some of the hot coffee. It felt good after a night in the freezing rain and snow. "You know, it could be Chandler is right. Maybe somebody else *is* behind the trouble here. Maybe somebody wants you to think it's Chandler."

"Playing both ends against the middle?" Lucinda said.

"It's happened before."

"But who could be doing it?"

Sam drank more coffee. "One or two of the small ranchers working together, maybe. Somebody from town. It could be anybody. Rustling's a profitable game."

"But if it is Clay?"

Sam was grim. "He's been warned what to expect."

"What are you going to do next?"

"I've got some ideas. I'll likely be gone a few days."

"Where?"

Sam nodded upstream, toward the high country. "I'm going to start up at the lake. If there's an organized band of rustlers in the Basin, they must have a headquarters some-where—besides at their home ranch, or in town, or wherever they're from. Lake McKenzie would be a good place. There's water and grazing, and it's remote from the other ranches."

Lucinda smiled. "I remember when you were young, you used to talk about starting a place of your own up there."

"It's where I'd go if I was a rustler."

Lucinda hesitated. "Sam, will I see you again? I mean, you're not going to clear up this trouble then leave the Basin, are you? Not with-out saying goodbye?"

Sam reached down and smoothed her black hair. It seemed like only yesterday that she had been taller than he, and he'd looked up to her—in more ways than one. It seemed like yesterday, and it seemed like an eternity ago. "You'll see me again," he promised. "I'll be back by the start of the roundup."

She looked relieved. "Good. You know, you . . . you haven't thought about staying on in the Basin have you? I mean, after this is over?"

"Lucy, there's a price on my head. There's probably folks hunting me right now."

"We could get your murder charge dismissed. It *was* self-defense, you know, and . . ."

Sam put a finger on her lips, stopping her. "I never wanted to leave," he said. "But let's worry about that later. You get on back to the ranch, before you get in more trouble than you already are."

Lucinda untied Honeysuckle from the hackberry bush to which he was tethered. She fiddled with the reins for a second, then she looked into Sam's eyes. "Be careful, Sam."

"I will, Big Sister." Sam swatted her bottom playfully with his hat. "Now you get going."

Lucinda mounted and rode out, leading Sam's old horse. Sam finished the pot of coffee and changed into the dry clothes. Then he saddled the fresh horse and started off.

It was past midday when he reached Lake McKenzie. The lake was huge, its deep blue water surrounded by green meadows and stands of lodgepole pine and golden aspens. The lake's surface was thick with migrating trumpeter swans, and their raucous honking filled the air. Sam was going to have a big job; it would take a day just to ride around the lake. He sighed and got started.

He rode southeast, away from the prevailing winds. He swung back and forth, hoping to cut a recent trail. He found an abandoned ranch, built and deserted in the years since he'd lived in the Basin, but there was no recent construction, no tracks of horses or cattle beyond that of a few strays. Several times Sam had the sensation that he was being followed. The sensation was so strong that once he laid up to watch his back trail, but no one appeared there, so he shrugged off the feeling and kept going. His nerves must be getting to him, he decided.

At dusk Sam made camp deep in a pine grove. The wind had picked up and the temperature was falling again. Sam debated whether to build a fire. He didn't want anyone knowing he was here. At last he found an embankment that would shelter the flame.

He made a fire, then sat near it, grateful for its warmth. He had not slept last night, and he felt drained. He made coffee and fried jerky and flapjacks in a small pan. Then he placed his rifle by his side, rolled himself in his blanket, and went to sleep.

The Apache in him brought him awake. It was the middle of the night. He felt a terrible urgency. He rolled from his blanket, grabbing his rifle, without really knowing why he was doing it. As he did, there was an earsplitting roar, accompanied by a bright flash. The bullet tore into the blanket roll Sam had just vacated. As Sam dove into the darkness of the trees, there was another shot and flash, and the bullet clipped a pine branch over his head.

Wide awake now, Sam fired his rifle in the

direction of the flashes, atop the embankment, then moved to avoid any return fire. But there was no return fire. Sam heard footsteps running through the woods—it sounded like one man. Sam jumped up, climbed the embankment, and started after, running heedlessly in the darkness, barefoot over rocks and uneven ground. He followed the retreating footsteps, then stopped. He heard hoofbeats galloping away. Frustrated, he raised his rifle and fired twice in the direction of the noise even though he knew there was no chance of hitting anything.

The hoofbeats faded into the darkness, and Sam swore. That two-thousand-dollar reward on his head must have come home to roost. Who had shot at him? The truth was, it could have been almost anybody. Whoever it had been, Sam doubted that he'd be back tonight.

Sam made his way through the pines back to his camp. He moved his blanket roll away from the fire, deep into the shadows. He laid down and wrapped himself up once more, but for the rest of the night he could not sleep.

CHAPTER 15

RAIN AND MELTED SNOW HAD TURNED Buffalo Notch's single street into a morass. The horses of the small ranchers splashed mud on their own legs and bellies and on the legs of their riders as they entered town. People stopped to watch the little group as it rode past. There were ten riders and a wagon to carry the supplies. The ranchers were nervous, hoping to avoid trouble. They had elected not to bring sidearms into town, only their saddle guns. Every spread in the Basin was represented, either by its owner or by one of the hands—every spread but one.

"I wish Jack was with us," said the pudgy

cowboy called Biscuit, who hired out to the various outfits as he was needed.

"He said he was too 'sick,' to come," young Tom Singer recalled unhappily. "If he don't lay off that bottle, he'll be too sick for the roundup, as well."

The lanky rancher Pete Fleming was more tolerant. "Guess he was celebrating too much. He's probably happy that bounty hunter left. I know I wouldn't want a fellow like that staying in my house."

Big, bearded Mike Kennedy said, "Don't be so sure. A fellow like that might come in handy, the way things have been going."

"He wasn't much good against us the other night," Fleming rejoined, and a couple of the men laughed.

Sid Allison, the ex-cavalryman, said, "How do we know that Slater *did* leave? I wouldn't be surprised if he ain't joined up with Chandler by now."

Kennedy agreed. "Be more his line, you'd think."

Biscuit said, "It hard to believe, Miss Lucinda having that kind of man for a cousin."

The party halted in front of Simpson's General Merchandise and Grocery. The wagon was braked, the horses hitched, and the men paraded inside, spurs jingling. One side of the store was lined with shelves and barrels, filled with food and dry goods; the other side, like most buildings in town, had a makeshift bar. The cattlemen bought supplies of flour, bacon, sugar, coffee, rope, and ammunition and loaded them on the wagon.

"Thirsty work," Tom Singer said when they were done. "Let's go back in for a drink."

Kennedy said, "I don't know. Maybe that ain't such a good idea. I don't like staying in town any longer'n we have to."

"Oh, what can happen?" chided Tom. "We're just getting a few drinks."

Most of the men agreed with Tom. "Come on," said the red-haired cowboy called Phil, who worked for Kennedy. "It's a warm day, and we got us a long ride back."

Kennedy gave in. "All right."

The cowmen crossed the room and bellied up to the bar, while Simpson came from behind the merchandise counter to serve them. There were only three other men in the bar—two of Chandler's cowboys, in town on some errand; and a small, dark fellow in leather workingman's garb, who had wandered in while the cattlemen were loading the wagon.

The cattlemen got a round of beers and whiskeys, tilted back their hats, and drank. Chandler's men looked at them but said nothing. They were too outnumbered to start trouble. The small man stared at the ranchers curiously.

At last he spoke to them with some kind of European accent. "There certainly are a lot of you. You just about double the population of this town."

Downing another round of drinks, the ranchers laughed. The small man went on. "Are you what they call cowboys?"

"Sort of," replied Boyer. He added, "I ain't seen you around here before. What kind of work you do?"

"A bit of this, a bit of that. Are you from the big ranch everyone talks about?"

Kennedy said, "The Lazy H? No, we're from the other spreads."

A knowing smile crossed the small man's dark face. "Oh, yes. You are the—'rustlers' is the word, isn't it? I have heard about you."

Pete Fleming looked at the small man sourly. "Somebody's been telling you lies, mister."

"Come, now. I'm not the police. You needn't pretend. I don't care that you steal cows for a living."

Fleming poured another drink. "Big words from a little man."

The small man's face took on a wounded look. He glanced around the room, as if seeking support. "You think because I'm little, you're better than me?"

"I'm sure a hell of a lot bigger," Fleming joked. He and some of his friends laughed.

The little man spread his hands in frustration. "All my life, I must listen to this. I am little, so people think they are better than me. Even rustlers, I can't believe it."

Fleming pushed away from the bar. "I said we ain't rustlers. Now let it rest, midget."

Simpson, the store owner, said, "Come on now, boys. I don't want any trouble."

"Don't be so hot headed," Kennedy told Fleming, grabbing his arm.

Fleming shrugged Kennedy off. He walked over to the small man, looked at him with disdain. "I could put you in my pocket—and still have room for a plug of tobacco."

The small man remained calm. "That is where you put the stolen cows—in your pocket?"

Fleming hit the small man on the jaw and sent him reeling along the bar. The small man tried to recover, but Fleming moved in on him with a left and a right that knocked him to the floor. The small man rolled across the floor, putting distance between himself and Fleming. As the cowman came after him, the small man reached into his coat with a lightning-quick movement and drew out a pistol. He fired three shots so close together that they almost sounded like one.

Fleming staggered backward, a surprised look on his face, blood already showing on his chest. Then he lost his balance, like a drunken man, and fell on his back. Twitching slowly, he gurgled and coughed up a spray of blood. Then the twitching stopped and he lay still, his hands drawn up clawlike by his shoulders. The surprised look was still on his face.

The other cattlemen knelt around their fallen friend. "Jesus," breathed Sid Allison, "he's dead." Through the spreading blood on Fleming's chest they saw that the three bullets had struck home in a group whose diameter was no bigger than that of a silver dollar.

The small man rose to his feet, wild-eyed, flourishing the pistol at the cattlemen. "Do any more of you wish to fight?" he shouted.

He started toward the ranchers, but Chandler's two cowboys held him back. "Come on, Branko. That's enough."

"Branko!" said Matt Taverner.

Branko pointed the pistol at Taverner. "You do not like my name?"

Taverner put up his hands. "No. No. It's fine."

Tom Singer said, "Somebody better get Marshal Cummings."

Simpson, the store owner, said, "He's out of town. He went hunting with some friends."

Tom swore. Kennedy said to Branko, "Why'd you have to shoot him?"

"Self-defense—what do you think? He was going for his gun."

Kennedy moaned. "He didn't have a gun. None of us do."

Kennedy looked to Simpson, the only impartial witness in the room.

"I admit, it looked like self-defense to me," Simpson said.

"Chandler has bought you, too, hasn't he?" Kennedy charged.

"I'm just telling what I saw."

Branko was grinning now. "You cow stealers had better go away from here."

"We're going," Boyer told him.

Boyer and Kennedy carried Fleming's body outside, followed by the rest of the cattlemen. There was a crowd around the store, watching. While Boyer and Kennedy laid the body in the wagon bed and covered it with a tarp, red-haired Phil stared at the horses lined along the hitch rail, with the loaded rifles in their scabbards. Phil turned to his friend Biscuit and the others. "What do you say—want to get our rifles and go back in there?"

Before any of the cattlemen could answer, Branko's voice said, "I would not try it, boys."

The cattlemen turned to see themselves covered by Branko and a half dozen of Clay Chandler's gunmen, weapons in hand, who seemed to have been conjured up out of nowhere.

"We've been set up," Kennedy realized. "This was a trap, and we walked right into it."

Branko laughed. "How clever of you to figure it out. Now get out of town, you fools. Get out of this Basin."

The cattlemen mounted and started out of town, saddened by Pete Fleming's death and burning with humiliation.

"Damn," swore Sid Allison. "Jack should have been here. He would have known what to do."

"Maybe," said Tom Singer. "Maybe not."

Allison turned in the saddle. "What are you saying, Tom?"

"Nothing. It's just funny how Jack ain't here when we need him, that's all."

Boyer waved him off. "Don't be silly. He had a bad hangover, that's all."

"It ain't the first he's had, neither," added Kennedy.

Tom didn't look convinced. The men kept going.

One by one, the cattlemen scattered to their homes as they proceeded northwest up the Basin. Those remaining, plus Tom Singer, who insisted on accompanying them, reached the Mitchell ranch late that afternoon. Lucinda was not there, but they told Jack what had happened in town.

"I can't take any more of this," said Sid Allison. "I'm beat."

"Me, too," added Mike Kennedy reluctantly.

"What do you mean?" Jack asked them.

Tom Singer explained. "We're quitting, Jack. There's not going to be any roundup. There's not going to be any more ranching—not in the Arrowhead Basin, anyway."

Allison added, "We're fighting a battle we can't win. We're pulling out."

Jack looked around the circle of drained faces. "You're all agreed?"

"We are," said Allison. "Chandler has won."

"No," Jack swore. "Not by a long shot he hasn't. Go on and quit, then. Lucinda and me will have our own roundup. We'll make a trail herd and take it to Miles City by ourselves. Go on, leave. We don't need you."

Kennedy said, "Don't be crazy, Jack. That's suicide. You can't fight Chandler by yourself."

"Watch me."

Jack's friends prepared to continue their argument, when they were distracted by hoof-beats, coming hard. They turned to see Lucinda riding toward them. She crossed the stream, then pulled up in front of the house, carrying some kind of paper in her hand.

"I was out riding near Lake McKenzie," she said, breathless. "On my way back, I found one of our steers killed—butchered—just over the hill there. Somebody had pinned this to its carcass."

She handed the note to Jack. The other ranchers gathered around as he read the crude scrawl: RUSTLER—MITCHELL. LEAVE THIS BASIN IN FORTY-EIGHT HOURS. OR ELSE. it was signed: THE COMMITTEE OF TWENTY.

CHAPTER 16

UNSUCCESSFUL AT LAKE MCKENZIE, SAM headed for the far end of the Basin. He reasoned that was where the rustlers, if there were rustlers, must be taking out the stock. It was rugged country, uninhabited; it would be easy to bring through small herds of cattle without being noticed. Once out of the Basin, the rustlers would be close to the mining camps like Helena, Bannack, and Virginia City, where beef brought prime prices.

But no headquarters in the Basin meant—what? Probably that the rustling was being carried out by small groups, men who got in quick and left the same way. That would seem to absolve Clay Chandler, and any of the other ranchers in the Basin. If it was an organized gang—and because of the killings, Sam had to assume that it was—they must be headquartered outside the Basin.

He rode northwest, with the mountains, heavy with snow after the recent storm, looming before him. This was high country. The aspen leaves, just turning color lower down, were past their peak up here. Many had already fallen and were floating in the streams; others drifted past Sam on the chill breeze. It was rugged country, as well. In some places you could see for fifty miles; in others you couldn't see five hundred feet.

The Arrowhead branched up here, into several small streams. After a few false starts, Sam found what he was looking for. A much-used trail bearing the tracks of cattle.

He followed the trail, which paralleled one of the streams, until he came to a spot where another trail entered it—one that had been made that day. Sam dismounted and examined this new trail. There had been about sixty to seventy head of cattle, along with five riders. And the horse of one rider had a v-shaped nick in the shoe of its near foreleg. This was the same bunch that had hanged Jud Pratt. When they had gone onto Chandler's land afterward, it must have been to steal cattle. Chandler must have been telling the truth.

Sam smiled grimly to himself and kept on.

Late in the afternoon, he topped a wooded ridge. Below him was a clearing with what looked like an old line cabin. The herd of cattle was there, bedded down in the clearing, and the five men were preparing to make camp. Smoke rose from the cabin's chimney.

Sam led his horse down the reverse side of the ridge and unsaddled him. He rubbed him down and fed him, then set him out to graze, while he himself ate a cold meal of jerky and biscuits. Later he staked out the horse, then he took his rifle and climbed back over the ridge, where he assumed a position in sight of the cabin and settled in for the night.

Dawn came, and the little valley was thick with fog. Everything was unnaturally quiet; the millions of tiny droplets suspended in the air provided a cushion that absorbed all sound. Sam crept down the ridge toward the cabin. He carried his rifle, and his pistol was loose in its holster. He was wet and chilled after a night in the open, but the prospect of action warmed him.

The cattle were ghostly shapes in the fog. A few had risen, but most stayed bedded down. Sam eased his way close to them, speaking softly to them in Apache. They lowed and shied out of his way, but they didn't bolt. Sam was surprised to see brands besides Chandler's represented in the little herd—there was the S Bar S, Kennedy's Four 8's, and plenty of others he didn't recognize. The horses in the tumbledown corral remained quiet. With the fog and the absence of a breeze, they hadn't smelled Sam.

Sam reached the cabin. He listened at the door, but heard only low snores. He felt no remorse for what he was about to do to these men. He doubted they would have felt any for him. They sure hadn't felt any for Jud Pratt.

He gave the door a push; it opened with a creak and he stepped in. In the dim light he could just make out the men on the floor, wrapped in blankets. A sleepy voice said, "Who's that?"

Sam knew they would fight, but he had to give them a chance. "Give up, I've got you covered."

The inside of the cabin became a blur as the rustlers scrambled out of their blankets and went for their guns. Coolly, Sam opened up with his Winchester, sweeping the small cabin from left to right, dropping four of the rustlers before they were half aware what had hit them. He went to one knee beside the last man, grabbing the man's hair with one hand, drawing his pistol with the other hand and ramming it under the man's jaw, forcing his head back painfully. The man was wide-eyed, terrified of this scarred apparition who had suddenly appeared before him.

The dimly lit cabin was thick with powder smoke and fog drifting in the open door. Somewhere a dying man groaned. The man who Sam held was young; he might have been nice looking if his teeth hadn't been so bad. "You ever fight Apaches?" Sam asked him in a gritty voice.

The man shook his head as well as he was able with the pistol barrel jammed under his jaw. "N-no. Never."

"Well, a soldier I once talked to, he told me that when the army catches a bunch of Apaches what they like to do is kill them all but one. They save that one for questioning. They figure he'll see the bodies of his friends and get the hint." Sam pulled harder on the man's hair. "Do *you* get the hint?"

"Yeah," the man gulped. "I get it."

"Good. What's your name?"

"Thomas. Harold Thomas."

"Where are you from?"

"Texas, by way of Ogallala and Miles City."

"You and your friends stole those cattle out there, didn't you?"

"Yeah."

"You also pretended to be deputy marshals and hung Jud Pratt?"

Thomas tried to get away from the pressure of the pistol barrel, but couldn't. "That's—that's right."

"Clay Chandler will be interested to hear what you just said."

"It was Clay Chandler that paid me to steal them."

Sam drew back the pistol a fraction; he eased his grip on the man's hair. "Chandler paid you to steal his own cows?"

"That's right. It's so's he can claim they're being rustled. We sell his cows in Bannack; the money goes into a bank account he has there. The money from the other cows he lets us keep for ourselves."

Prime steers would go for twenty-five, maybe thirty, dollars a head in the mining camps. Sixty to seventy head at that price represented a tidy sum. "And Jud Pratt—did Chandler pay you for that job, too?"

"Yeah, two hundred a man. Branko ran the operation."

"Branko. I've heard that name."

"Well you don't want to meet the man. He's a mean one."

"So am I," Sam said. Then he added, "I should have killed Chandler when I had the chance." He stood, motioning with the pistol. "All right, get up."

Thomas was scared as he rose. "You going to let me live?"

"I said I would if you talked."

Thomas looked relieved. "Thanks."

"Don't thank me. It was business."

"Look—since you played square with me—I know something else."

"What?"

"One of the ranchers is working for Chandler."

Sam frowned. "Who?"

"I don't know his name. I've only heard his voice. He meets Chandler from time to time, to tell him what the ranchers are doing."

Sam wiped a hand across his mouth. "Would you know this man's voice if you heard it again?"

"Sure."

"Will you come with me and identify him?"

"You said I could go."

Sam let out his breath. "Yes, I did, and I meant it. But this is important. I'll have to insist."

"But the ranchers. When they find out who I am, what I've done, they'll—"

"No, they won't. I give you my word on that, and I don't go back on my word. Once you've identified the man, you'll be free to go. I might even be able to arrange some money for you."

Thomas hesitated, then he said, "What the hell. Why not?"

Sam started outside. Thomas looked back at the men on the floor. "What about them? Some of them ain't dead yet."

"They will be," Sam assured him.

Before leaving, Sam cut loose the rustlers' remaining horses from the corral. Someone would find them and the stolen cattle eventually. Thomas saddled his horse then gave Sam a ride over the ridge, where Sam picked up his own horse.

Sam and Harold Thomas started back down the Basin. The fog was burning off with the promise of an unusually warm, sunny day. Thomas said, "I said I'd go with you, but don't go thinking you'll get me to testify before no jury."

"This isn't going to come to a jury," Sam told him.

"You intend to kill Chandler?"

"I intend to try."

The trail ran alongside a shallow, rocky stream. All around the hills pressed close, thick with autumn foliage, with the smells of leaves and berries—and something else, something musty. Sam stiffened, coming alert.

As he did, the slope on one side of the stream erupted with flame and the roar of gunshots. Thomas and his horse were hit and went down. Sam's horse was hit and reared. It was hit again, in the neck, and it fell, spraying Sam with gouts of bright red arterial blood. Sam hit his head and lay stunned, while more bullets splashed the water around him.

Then there was silence. The birds began singing again, as if nothing had happened. Sam was in the open. If he tried to get up and run for cover he'd be cut down by the unseen men above him. He could tell from the strangled moans nearby that Thomas was hit bad. Thomas had been closer to the gunfire; his body had taken most of the bullets meant for Sam. Whoever the ambushers were, they were not very good. An experienced leader, or one with half a brain, would have placed men on both sides of the stream. Sam owed his life to someone's stupidity. Still, he was not out of this yet.

He lay on his side in the freezing water, feigning death. His pistol was out of the water, his hand near its butt. He would have to be patient, try to catch them off guard. After a moment, he heard whispers up the hill, then the crackling of underbrush as the shooters made their cautious way down.

"Are they dead?" asked a voice.

"Looks like," replied another, and Sam recognized the voice as that of Marshal Cummings.

"Which one's Slater?"

"The one on the far side," said Cummings.

Through half-opened eyes, Sam observed them as they came into view. Besides Marshal Cummings, there were three others. Two had the look of buffalo hunters. That was what Sam had smelled before—buffalo. They couldn't wash the smell off—not that they looked like they'd washed off much of anything recently. The buffalo were gone, so they had decided to hunt men. The fourth man was one of the small ranchers—Miles Masterson, who must have delayed his exit from the Basin and turned bounty hunter out of greed.

"Who's t'other one?" said one of the buffalo hunters.

Cummings bent over Harold Thomas's body. "He worked for Clay Chandler."

"What's he doing with Slater?"

"Damn if I know."

Miles Masterson was hopeful. "Maybe there's a reward on him, too?"

"If we're lucky," answered the marshal.

The men lowered their weapons. "Shame about the horses," said the second buffalo hunter. "We coulda sold them."

"You can't have everything," Cummings told him. "Be grateful for what you're going to make off Slater."

The four men steered around Thomas's still thrashing horse and moved close to Sam, convinced he was dead. "Damn," said the first buffalo hunter, awestruck. "Lookit all that blood."

At that moment, Sam rose from the stream, drawing his pistol in the same motion. Marshal Cummings dropped his jaw. Sam shot him first, in the chest. Looking like he'd seen a ghost, the first buffalo hunter turned and ran. Miles Masterson had more grit. He raised his rifle and was trying to fire, when Sam's bullet drilled him in the forehead. The other buffalo hunter squeezed off a wild shot, then he, too, turned to run. Sam's shot caught him in the back, knocking him face first into the water. Sam fired after the other retreating buffalo hunter, but with the pistol's limited range, he missed. Cursing, he picked up Cummings's Henry repeater and fired that, but the man was in the trees by now, and Sam couldn't get a good shot. The buffalo hunter disappeared over the hill. A few minutes later Sam heard the sound of departing horses. The would-be killer had the good sense to take all the mounts with him, to keep Sam from using one to chase after him.

Sam stood in the icy water of the stream, looking at all the senseless death. Was one of these men the same one who had shot at him the other night while he camped? He didn't think so.

"I must be a popular fellow," he said to himself.

He looked at Harold Thomas. If Thomas hadn't volunteered his information about the traitor, Sam wouldn't have made him come along. If Thomas hadn't come along, in all likelihood Sam would now be lying dead in the stream and Thomas would be riding away a free man. Life was funny.

Now that Thomas was dead, Sam had no one

who could identify Chandler's spy among the ranchers. Sam reloaded his pistol, then took his Winchester and saddlebags from his dead horse. He threw his saddlebags over his shoulder and started the long walk back to Lucinda's house.

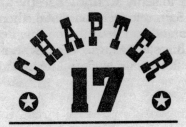

CHAPTER 17

BRANKO PESIC RODE FROM BUFFALO NOTCH toward the Lazy H Ranch. He rode awkwardly, unused to horses. He was a man of the mountains, where travel was conducted mainly by foot.

Branko was from Serbia, a rugged country in the Balkan region of eastern Europe. It was a land of violent, passionate people, among whom Branko had stood out by his hotheaded courage and willingness—even eagerness—to kill. These qualities had won him employment in the dynastic squabbles and intrigues that rent his kingdom. When it was discovered that he was using his talents to serve both sides in the struggle, he had been forced to flee his native country for the United States.

He had landed in New York, where he quickly put his talents to use. He had joined the Rats, one of the most vicious gangs in the Five Points area of the city. Then he had run into trouble with the law and had been forced to flee once again, this time heading west, where ability with a gun was always in demand.

He had ended up in Deadwood, working for the ring of gamblers and pimps who ran the town. He had held the original contract on Bill Hickok's life, until that drunken fool Tom McCall beat him to it. But, inevitably, the law had come to Deadwood. The good times were ending. Branko had been ready to move on when he was approached by Clay Chandler. Branko enjoyed working for Chandler, but the job was almost over now. Soon it would be time to move on once more. Branko was getting used to that. He was starting to imagine that this was what the rest of his life would be like.

He rode into the yard by the ranch house. "Where is Mister Chandler?" he asked a passing cowboy.

The cowboy, a working hand who had no use for Branko, hooked a thumb. "Over to the tack shed."

Branko rode over. He found Chandler sitting

in front of the shed with some of the other hands, mending saddles and harness in preparation for the gathering of cattle—"roundup," they called it—which would start soon.

Chandler was restitching the cantle of his saddle. He looked up as Branko approached. "I have news," Branko said, dismounting.

Chandler put down his saddle and tools, and the two men moved out of earshot of the other hands. Branko said, "The policeman Cummings is dead."

Chandler shrugged. "So?"

"Sam Slater killed him."

Chandler stopped walking. "You're sure?"

"I heard in town. One of those buffalo hunters that Cummings took with him to kill Slater came back. The others are all dead. This one stopped just long enough to get a fresh horse and get out of the Basin."

Chandler was unconcerned with the surviving buffalo hunter's fate. "Where did this happen?"

"At the northwest end of the Basin. The buffalo hunter said there was a man with Slater. He said the man worked for you."

Chandler frowned.

"Who could it have been?" Branko asked.

"Up there? It must have been Thomas or one of his crew."

"You think that Slater learned the truth about what you are doing?"

"Who knows what he learned?" Chandler replied irritably.

Chandler looked away. Following Slater's nighttime visit to the ranch, Chandler had been found by his men the next morning and released. Branko's news was the first indication he'd had of Slater's whereabouts since then.

Chandler had lied his way out of that confrontation with Slater, and the truth was, Slater had spooked the hell out of him, the way he'd been able to sneak right onto the ranch. Chandler wasn't scared of any man, but Slater was . . . there was something different about him.

Whenever Chandler returned to his house at night now, he did so cautiously, with his hand on his gun—and he made sure that he always carried a gun these days. He would have slept in the bunkhouse with the men, but he couldn't let them see that he was scared. He had put on night guards and more dogs, but he didn't think that would stop Slater if he chose to return. It didn't matter. The next time they met, it was going to be on Chandler's terms.

He turned back to Branko. "Did you deliver that note to the Mitchells?"

"I did. Do you think it will work?"

"No. Mitchell won't run. I wish he *would* run, because if he did, Lucinda wouldn't, and that would make things easier for me. No, the note was just to be on record that the Committee of Twenty is watching Mitchell."

"Ah, yes, the famous Committee of Twenty. Their identity is such a mystery."

"It's you, me, and about eighteen of those fellows." Chandler pointed to the bunkhouse, where his hired guns lounged. "Of course the law will never know that."

Branko grinned.

"Mitchell's the last," Chandler said. "They've all quit but him. Once he's eliminated, the Basin is ours."

"Yours," corrected Branko politely.

"Point taken, Mister Pesic. We won't be able to trick Mitchell like we did Pratt, and I doubt we can ambush him the way we did Singer."

"If we attack his house, there is a danger of hurting his wife."

"No," said Chandler. "I'll kill the man that hurts her. Hell, I'm doing this for her. We'll have to get her out of the way first."

"How do we do that?"

Chandler smiled. "I think it's time to play our hole card."

"And after that, we take care of Slater?"

"Exactly. That's a meeting I'm looking forward to."

CHAPTER 18

SAM RETURNED TO THE MITCHELL RANCH late the next afternoon. It had been a long walk, but Sam was used to long walks. He came up the stream with long, easy strides, the saddle-bags over his shoulder and the Winchester in his hand.

The dogs sounded a warning. They had gotten used to him, but they must have smelled the dried horse's blood that covered him. In front of Sam the house looked different. It was boarded up, like the occupants were expecting trouble.

Then the front door opened and Lucinda appeared, her black hair pinned back. "Sam!"

She ran off the porch to meet him. "Sam, I'm so glad you're . . ."

She stopped, staring at his bloodstained clothes. "Sam, are you all right?"

"Yeah."

"Oh, thank God." She hugged him, and he held her in his arms, kissing her forehead. He looked up to see Jack watching from the door.

"I was afraid that Clay's men had gotten you, too," Lucinda told him.

"'Too'?" asked Sam. "Has somebody else been killed?"

"Pete Fleming."

"The one that beat me up?"

"Yes. It happened in Buffalo Notch. That man called Branko goaded Pete into a fight, then shot him."

"Couldn't Jack have stopped it?"

"Jack didn't go to town. He was . . . sick."

"You mean hungover."

She didn't answer. She didn't have to. Sam pursed his lips.

Lucinda went on, "Now we've received a warning note from the Committee of Twenty telling us to be off the land by tomorrow."

That explained why the house was boarded up. "Are you leaving?" Sam asked.

She gave him a dirty look. "This is our land, and nobody is going to run us off it." Despondently, she added, "The other ranchers have quit. Pete Fleming's death was the last straw for them. Jack and I are the only ones left." Sam nodded, and she said, "What happened to you?"

"I found the men that hung Jud Pratt." He told her about Thomas and his men, and what he had learned about Chandler's rustling operation.

"So Clay was lying to you?"

"Yeah. I figured he was, but I couldn't do anything till I was sure. I learned something else. One of your friends is working for Chandler."

"What?" she said. "You mean one of the small ranchers?"

"Thomas, one of the fellows that killed Pratt, knew about it. He could only identify the man by his voice. I was bringing him back here to do just that, when I got jumped by a bunch of amateur bounty hunters led by Marshal Cummings and your friend Miles Masterson."

"Miles!" said Lucinda, surprised and saddened that someone she knew so well would have stooped to such an act.

Sam went on. "Thomas got killed, and I got these bloodstains."

"What happened to Miles and the marshal?"

"Let's just say I'm here and they're not. What are your plans now that the other ranchers have quit?"

"I'm not sure. Jack and I have barely spoken

since that night he had you beaten up. I think he wants to try and take a small herd to Miles City anyway, but I'm afraid that if we do that, Clay will burn us out while we're gone or just ambush us on the trail and kill us. I'd rather fort up and fight it out here. What about you, do you have a plan?"

"I promised Chandler I'd pay him another visit if he lied to me."

"He'll be waiting for you."

"He'll have good reason."

Lucinda changed the subject. "Come inside. You must be tired and cold. I'll get you something to eat."

Sam grinned. "To tell the truth, I've got a hankering for one of your chokeberry pies."

"I've got some berries picked. I'll make you one if you don't mind waiting."

"I don't mind at all."

Arms around each other, they walked back to the ranch house. Jack was inside, glaring at them from over a tin cup full of whiskey. "I'm surprised you'd show your face around here again, Slater."

"Jack, don't start," Lucinda warned.

Sam said, "Let him talk, Lucy. Talking seems to be what he's good at."

Jack's eyes narrowed suspiciously. "What do you mean by that?"

"You know what I mean. One of the ranchers

has been working with Chandler, telling him your every move. I think it's you."

Jack looked at Lucinda, then back at Sam again. "You're crazy."

"Why? You're as good a choice as any. You never seem to be around when there's trouble."

Jack saw an element of doubt cross Lucinda's face. He said, "I don't have to listen to this. But then it's no more than I'd expect from a man who's come all this way to make love to my wife."

Sam lowered his voice. "I'm getting tired of hearing you say that."

"So what? It's the truth. Every time I turn around I find you two falling over each other, sneaking off together like a couple of dogs in heat."

"Jack!" said Lucinda.

"She's in love with you. And you're in love with her."

Sam said, "She's my cousin, you fool."

"I don't care what she is. I know what I see."

"It's hard to see anything through the bottom of a bottle."

Jack dropped his cup and slugged Sam in the jaw, knocking him backward. San threw down his rifle and saddlebags.

"Stop it!" Lucinda told them.

"It's all right," Sam said. To Jack he said, "I've been meaning to pay you back for the other . . ."

Jack threw another punch. Sam blocked it, and replied with a left and right to the face that staggered Jack backward into the cupboard. Plates and cups crashed to the floor, shattering. Jack came off the cupboard with a bull-like rush. Sam hit him flush on the nose with a right, but Jack's momentum carried him into Sam's midriff, and they went over a chair, breaking it. They got to their feet, still locked together, banging around the small room, knocking things over, hurting themselves on the heavy furniture, punching, scratching, trying to trip each other. At last they smashed through the partly open front door, knocking it from its leather hinges as they stumbled out onto the porch and fell off it, into the dust.

Sam pushed Jack away and stood. Jack got up, as well. The two men circled, fists raised, breathing hard. Lucinda came out onto the porch after them. "Will you stop?" she pleaded, but they paid no attention.

Sam moved right, away from Jack's powerful right hand. With his left, Sam hit Jack under the left eye, snapping his head back. He hit him again, and again, then he stepped back as Jack threw a roundhouse right that just grazed his cheek. Jack followed with a left that missed entirely, and the two men drew back, circling again.

Sam hit Jack's eye again, making him grunt with pain. Jack threw a right. Sam ducked it, hit

him a left in the gut and followed with an over-
hand right to the jaw that knocked him backward. As Sam moved in to follow his advantage
Jack recovered and caught him with a wicked
left hook to the temple that almost knocked him
off his feet.

They paused, catching their breath. There
was blood around Jack's nose, and a swelling
knot beneath his left eye. Sam's vision was
blurred from the blow to the temple. Blood trick-
led from his right eyebrow. He moved in again,
but this time Jack came first, with another rush.
Sam tried to dodge, but Jack caught him around
the waist with one hand and threw him heavily
to the ground. Jack jumped on Sam's back,
grinding Sam's face into the dirt as though he
were trying to rub it off. Sam couldn't breathe;
his mouth, nose, and eyes were full of dirt and
pebbles. With a furious effort, he rolled Jack off.
As he got to his knees, Jack grabbed him
around the neck with one hand, pounding his
face repeatedly with the other. Blindly, Sam
reached up and grabbed the back of Jack's hair.
He yanked on it as hard as he could, trying to
pull it out by its roots. Jack cried out with pain;
his grip on Sam lessened. Again blindly, Sam
reached up with his free hand and jabbed his
fingertips into Jack's exposed throat. Jack
gagged and fell back, and it was Sam's turn to
scramble on top of him, but Jack kicked up a

foot and Sam was forced to dodge it, throwing an ineffective punch as he did.

Both men climbed to their feet. Jack's left eye was closing, there was more blood under his nose. Sam's face felt like it had been sandpapered. It was bleeding from a thousand tiny cuts and scratches. Both men's shirts were torn. They sucked in great gulps of air.

"Can't you two stop now?" Lucinda yelled from the porch, but it had gone beyond that. This had to be settled.

Sam came forward in what seemed like slow motion. He feinted a blow to Jack's injured eye. Jack raised his arm to block it, and Sam went low and hit him twice in the gut. Jack doubled over, and Sam hit him with a grunting, two-fisted uppercut that knocked him back into the hitching rail in front of the house. He hit the rail hard and hung on. Sam lacked the strength to follow up.

Both men straightened with difficulty, staggering a bit to keep their balance, gulping down air. Jack pushed away from the hitch rail. He launched into another of his wild rushes. Sam stepped aside and threw Jack to the ground. Sam slipped and half fell himself.

Sam stood with his hands on his thighs, breathing hard. Jack tried to get up. As he did, Sam moved in and hit him with a clubbing left to the side of the head that sprawled him on his face in the dirt. He lay there and did not try to get up again. Sam collapsed to his knees in the dirt beside him.

Sam rolled Jack over and grabbed what was left of his shirt, lifting his head. "Now," he breathed, "like I said—Lucy's my cousin. I never . . . I never laid a hand on her. I never would."

Jack looked out of his good eye. There was blood all over his nose and swollen mouth. He spit some of the blood out and said weakly, "I still don't believe you."

"You son of a . . ." Sam raised his fist to hit the defenseless Jack again.

Then he heard Lucinda say, "Somebody's coming."

She was on the porch, staring out past the creek. Sam shoved Jack back to the ground and turned. In the late afternoon haze a dust cloud showed where a rider approached.

Sam stood, slowly. Jack tried, but he was unable. "It's Tom Singer," said Lucinda, shading her eyes against the setting sun.

The young man brought his horse at a good lope. He crossed the stream and reined in before the house. He looked at the two torn and bloody men, eyes widening as he recognized Sam.

"It's all right, Tom," Lucinda told him dryly. "They were just discussing the international situation. What brings you here so late in the day?"

Tom had a hard time keeping his eyes off Sam, but at last he said, "It's Hannah, Miss Lucinda. She's sick, and she needs help. She asked if I'd come fetch you."

"What's wrong with her?"

"I don't know. It's her stomach. All I know is she's hurting awful bad."

"And her with that baby," Lucinda said. "Sure, I'll go. Let me saddle Honeysuckle. You leave your horse in the barn and take one of ours."

"Yes, ma'am," said Tom, heading for the barn.

To Sam, Lucinda said, "I guess that pie will have to wait."

As Lucinda stepped off the porch, Sam took her arm. "I'll go with you."

"No," she said. "I'll be all right. You stay here and guard the ranch—if you and Jack don't kill each other first."

"I think we're done for the moment," Sam told her.

"I hope so."

Sam helped Lucinda saddle and bridle Honeysuckle. He held the horse for her while she mounted. "Be careful," he told her.

She smiled. "I will." Then she turned. "Come on, Tom."

Lucinda and Tom rode off in the fading autumn light, leaving Sam and Jack by themselves.

CHAPTER 19

LUCINDA AND TOM SINGER RODE THROUGH the gathering dusk and into the darkness. They took the shortcut across the line of hills that separated the Mitchells' valley from Three-Mile Creek. It was getting cold, and Lucinda wished she'd brought a heavier coat.

"Is Hannah conscious?" she asked Tom as their horses picked their way over the rough trail. "Is she able to care for the baby?"

"So far she is," Tom replied. "She's having a tough time, though."

"Matt Taverner is with her, I hope?"

"Yeah. He's there."

"The Boyer place is closer than ours, so is the Whitmans'. I'm surprised she didn't send you there."

Tom hesitated. "All I know is, she said she wanted you."

They topped the hill and started down the far side. Lucinda said, "Are you and Hannah still determined to leave the Basin, Tom?"

"Yes, ma'am. We are."

"Where will you go?"

"Don't rightly know."

"Winter's coming on. Think of the hardships you'll suffer."

"It's less of a hardship than being dead, I expect."

Lucinda said nothing more. They left the hills. They were about halfway to the Singers' place. The moon had come up, illuminating the vast ocean of rangeland before them. Suddenly Lucinda saw a group of mounted men leave the cover of an embankment and move to intercept them. She turned and saw another group emerging from the trees behind them.

"Tom, look!" she cried, pointing. "They're after us. Run for it!"

She started to wheel Honeysuckle to run for the open range, but Tom reached over and grabbed the horse's bridle, holding him in place.

"Tom, what are you doing?" Lucinda said.

Tom held the bridle firm. "Sorry, Miss Lucinda."

Lucinda looked at Tom in shock. "It's you, isn't it? You're the traitor."

Tom said nothing. Behind and before them, the shadowy men were coming on fast. Lucinda heard their horses pounding the turf.

"Tom, let go," she pleaded.

Tom refused, so Lucinda lashed him across the face with her reins. He yelped, and his grip on the bridle lessened. Lucinda yanked Honeysuckle free, wheeled him, and galloped off.

She headed east, toward the open range, but the men behind her had an angle. They were going to cut her off. She turned southeast. If she could make the next line of hills she could hide there. The first group of men had taken an interception angle, as well, so she veered slightly east again. If she could turn the corner on the lead group, she'd be home free. There wasn't a horse in the Basin that could catch Honeysuckle.

The lead riders came on, dark figures under the golden autumn moon. Lucinda lathered Honeysuckle with the reins's ends, keeping low in the saddle. She had already outdistanced the group behind her; there was only the group out front to beat. She turned the corner on them. Only the lead rider had a chance of catching her—it was Clay Chandler. He turned with her, trying for another interception angle, but he was not going to make it. She drew even with him. He tried to close, but she eased Honeysuckle away. She began to draw ahead. She had beaten him.

Then he drew his pistol. "Stop, Lucinda!" he shouted. "Stop, or I'll shoot your horse!"

Lucinda ground her teeth in frustration. She knew that Clay was serious, and she would almost rather die herself than see anything happen to Honeysuckle. She eased the tawny gelding to a lope, then a trot. As she did, Chandler rode in front of her, cutting her off. His men came up, cutting her off from behind and surrounding her.

Chandler holstered his pistol. Trying to appear casual, he leaned on his saddle pommel. "Evening, Miss Lucinda."

Like Chandler, Lucinda was breathing hard from the ride. "I take it this is not a social call," she said.

"Not exactly. No."

The rest of Chandler's men came up. There were about twenty of them altogether, heavily armed. She recognized some from around town. The one called Branko came last, riding stiffly. Tom Singer was there, too, looking guilty, and Lucinda turned to him. "Tom, how could you do this?"

Tom looked down, saying nothing.

"Hannah isn't sick, is she?"

Still there was no answer.

Lucinda went on. "You pretended to be sick,

so your own brother could go into Buffalo Notch and be killed. You told Clay that our men would be going into town, so that he could have his hired killer there waiting for them." (Branko smiled at that.) "God knows who else you've delivered up to this bunch. Now you've betrayed me, as well. What made you do it?"

"It's called money," Chandler told her. "And he got a lot of it."

Lucinda remembered how people had always said Tom was lazy, how he tried to get things without working for them, unlike his older brother. But he'd always been such a pleasant young man that she'd paid no notice.

To Chandler, she said, "What do you want with me, Clay?"

"We want to protect you," Chandler replied.

"From what?"

He smiled. "Well, from us, I guess."

Lucinda went cold inside. "Why, what are you planning to do?"

"We're going to clean out a nest of rustlers."

Lucinda gripped Honeysuckle's reins so hard that her knuckles showed white. There was no chance of getting away to warn the ranch. Her voice seemed to be coming from far away as she spoke. "And afterward? What will you do with me then?"

"Well . . . I was hoping you and me might eventually come to an . . . an understanding."

"Do you think you can kill my husband, then buy my love? You're mad."

Chandler straightened in the saddle. "Why do you think I've done all this, Lucinda? Why do you think I've worked myself to a nub, risked my life building an empire here? It's been for you. So that I'd be worthy of you, so that I could give you everything I couldn't give you before."

Lucinda sighed wearily. "It wasn't about what you could or couldn't give me, Clay—don't you see that? It was you. I didn't love you. I don't love you now. I never will love you."

"We'll see about that," Chandler said. Then he added, "If I can't have you, nobody will."

Tom Singer spoke up, "Mister Chandler?"

Chandler turned, "Yes?"

"You'd best know—Jack Mitchell ain't alone. That Slater fellow is with him."

"Is he?" Chandler said with interest.

"When I was there, it looked like the two of them had just finished one heck of a fistfight."

"So much the better," Chandler said. To Branko, he said, "Good news, Mister Pesic?"

Branko's interest was kindled. "Very good. What shall we do with the woman?"

"Let's bring her along. Who knows, she might prove useful."

CHAPTER 20

SAM AND JACK MITCHELL WERE ALONE IN the gathering dusk. Wearily, Sam sank onto the porch stoop. He looked at Jack lying in the dirt. Both men were bloody, their clothing torn.

"Why did you do it, Mitchell?" Sam asked. "Did Chandler give you money? Did he tell you he'd let you get away with your life? All the rest—these threats to you from the Committee of Twenty—they're just a smoke screen, aren't they?"

Jack looked up. His words sounded funny as he spoke out of his swollen mouth. "You'd like it if I was the traitor, wouldn't you, Slater? You'd like it if I was secretly working for Chandler. It would give you all the more excuse for chasing my wife."

Sam boiled with rage once more. He stood and moved away. If he stayed here he was likely to kill Jack. The only thing stopping him now was the fact that Jack was Lucy's husband.

He walked into the house, retrieved his rifle and saddlebags, then came back out and stood over Jack. "I'm spending the night in the barn. Don't try anything funny, or I'll forget you're family."

"I ain't family to you, Slater. Not now, not ever."

Sam restrained the urge to kick Jack's teeth down his throat. He walked away. It was just about dark now. By lamplight Sam fixed himself a bed of hay in the back corner of the barn, where he could cover the entrance. There used to be a little partitioned room for him here years ago, but that was gone. It was probably one of the first things Jack had gotten rid of.

He settled in, remembering the last night he had slept in this barn. He remembered how he'd been awakened by Lucy's screams. He remembered her struggling with his Uncle Henry. He remembered his own knife fight with his uncle, and how he'd been forced to flee afterward, a fugitive. He touched the long scar he'd gotten that night. He could almost feel it open again, feel his face awash with warm blood, the skin flapping against his cheek, and Lucy's tender touch as she sewed it closed. . . . His hand was shaking, the way it had shaken after he'd killed his uncle.

The world had changed for Sam that night. And now . . .

Now he didn't know. Things were so confused. He wondered if he had anything to fear from Jack during the night. He doubted it. Still, it paid to be prepared. He was almost tempted to camp outside somewhere, where he couldn't be found, but he was too tired and beaten up, and he wanted to be warm for a change. He laid his rifle and pistol beside him. He remembered that he hadn't had anything to eat. The hell with it, he'd eat in the morning. If he went over to the house now he'd have to look at Jack again, and he didn't think he was up to that. One of the dogs wandered in, a big yellow hunting dog named Vic. It sniffed around Sam, was petted, then snuggled in beside Sam with a contented groan, and the two of them went to sleep.

Outside the ranch house Jack Mitchell hauled himself painfully to his knees. It was dark now; crickets chirped. The moon was not yet up, and he couldn't see far. There was no sign of Slater; Jack supposed he was in the barn as he had promised. Jack blew clotted blood out of his nose, then he used the porch stoop as a crutch and pulled himself to his feet.

He was unsteady; his head hurt. He stepped up on the porch and went inside. He lit the lamp and trimmed it, then staggered across the room. He got his whiskey jug from the chair well, sat down, and drank.

The alcohol set the inside of his lacerated mouth on fire, and he spit it out, coughing with pain and surprise. After a second he tried again. It was a little better this time. He was able to swallow. After a few more jolts the inside of his mouth, as well as the rest of his body, were pleasantly numb. He sighed, leaned back, and closed his eyes.

Sometime during the night, the big yellow dog called Vic got up and left. Sam listened for a minute, then went back to sleep. Vic was probably off on some nocturnal jaunt, to check out a mysterious smell or noise, or on the kind of mission only a dog could fathom.

Soon Sam was awake again, alert this time. The rifle came into his hand as if by itself. Had he heard something? Yes, there it was again. It sounded like footsteps.

Carefully he sat up. His body was sore all over, and the movement produced a wave of pain, but he made himself ignore it. He listened closely. Men, a lot of them, were moving around the outbuildings—the bunkhouse, stable, and barn. These weren't friends, not at this time of night. He wondered why the dogs hadn't barked, but he couldn't worry about it right now.

There were more noises, from the barn entrance this time. Shadows moved against the moonlit entrance. At least two men were positioning themselves there, to cover the rear of the ranch house.

Sam thought about sneaking up behind the men and killing them, but there was no guarantee he could cross the dark barn without making noise. There was also no guarantee that there were only two men to deal with. Quietly he removed the spare ammunition from his saddlebags and stuffed it in his trouser pockets. He slipped on his high-topped moccasins. Then he stood and felt his way along the dark barn to the loft ladder. He reached it without alerting the men out front. He climbed, holding his rifle in one hand.

Near the top, one of the ladder rungs squeaked. From the front of the barn Sam heard urgent whispers. There was no time to stay put; Sam kept climbing. There was another squeak as he reached the top. Sam heard rifles being levered; someone was coming toward the rear.

Sam started across the loft floor. He tried to

be quiet, but dried hay slipped through cracks in the flooring, revealing his presence. "Somebody's up there," said a voice.

Sam said the hell with it. He started running for the loft window. Below him somebody began shooting. Bullets splintered the floor in a line behind Sam's feet.

Sam ran. The loft opening loomed large in the moonlight. Sam saw the pulley which was used to haul up bales of hay. He saw the rope tied securely around it. Below him the voices grew louder. He reached the opening, leaped, caught the rope, swung out and let go. He fell through the darkness, landing hard on the balls of his feet. The voices were right behind him. He picked himself up and started running for the house. "There he is!" cried somebody. "Get him!" Rifles opened up behind him, blasting the nighttime stillness, their orange spurts all around.

He ran straight, bent low. Bullets plucked at his sleeves and trouser legs. They whistled past his head and kicked up little spurts of dirt all around him. Then he reached the back of the house. He ran toward one of the boarded rear windows, lowered his shoulder, and dove through in an avalanche of splintered wood and breaking glass.

He hit the glass-covered floor and rolled. The men outside were still firing. He thrust his Winchester through what was left of the window and fired twice at the flashes to slow them up. In the front room a lamp was still burning. Jack Mitchell staggered through the doorway.

"Wha . . . ?" he mumbled thickly, reeking of whiskey. "What's going . . . ?"

"We're being attacked, you jughead," Sam said, giving him a shove. "Get a gun."

Sam turned back to the window. He had to hope that Jack could hold the front of the house. There were two windows at the house's rear. Sam went from one to the other, firing at the attackers, who were advancing now, running across the open ground. He heard screams and saw one man fall. Another stumbled, fell, then began crawling back to the stable. The rest of the attackers hesitated, then retreated to the cover of the outlying buildings.

In the front, Jack stumbled across the parlor. He pulled the shotgun from its resting place near the door. He kept the shotgun loaded for just such an emergency. Still half drunk, he threw open the front door, to be confronted with three men scrambling onto the porch. He fired both barrels of the shotgun. The three men collapsed in a heap, groaning. More men in the shadows ran away, firing back over their shoulders. Jack retreated into the house, slamming and barring the door. He crossed the room and blew out the lantern. Then he got his rifle from over the fireplace. He reloaded the shotgun and stood it by the door. He took the rifle and assumed a place by the boarded window.

From all sides of the ranch house, the attackers opened fire. Bullets smashed into walls and doors. They shattered the boards over the windows and the glass behind them. They splintered furniture inside the house. They smashed what was left of the crockery in the cupboard. The attackers were good shots. Even though the windows must be hard to see in the dark, they poured such a volume of accurate fire through them that Sam and Jack were unable to get off any return shots. Wistfully Sam remembered the old log cabin days, when you could just poke a hole in the wall's mud chinking and fight that way. In the stable the frightened horses were making a racket, kicking at their stalls.

Sam crawled into the front room, where Jack huddled against the wall. "Is it Chandler?" Jack asked above the noise of gunfire and splintering wood.

"Don't know who else it could be," Sam replied. Then he added, "I guess I was wrong about you working for him."

"Thanks," said Jack. "You can put that on my headstone."

Sam waited for Jack to say he had been wrong about Sam as well, but no such admission was forthcoming. Instead Jack said, "They almost surprised us. I wonder why the dogs didn't bark?"

"They set out poisoned meat, is my guess."

A look of disgust came over Jack for anyone who would do such a thing.

Sam said, "How are you fixed for ammunition?"

"I got plenty. I been expecting something like this to happen."

At that moment, a bullet hit the sheet-iron stove in the kitchen with a loud *bong* and ricocheted into the parlor, burying itself in the wall within an inch of Jack's head. "Damn," Jack said, his face paling. Then he added, "What do you think will happen?"

"They'll keep this up for a while, then rush us, probably at dawn."

"I'm glad Lucinda's not here."

They shared a look at the mention of her name. "Me, too," Sam said at last. "Keep your eyes open."

"Be hard to close them with all this racket going on."

Sam crawled back to the rear of the house. His head was showered with wooden splinters. A framed picture crashed to the floor near him, breaking the glass. The house was being shot to pieces. Sam went from window to window in the rear. The darkness was fading. Dawn was coming in, obscured by the bluish-gray fog of powder smoke that hung over the outbuildings and ranch house. The acrid smell tickled Sam's nose.

Suddenly the gunfire slackened and died. The only noises came from the dying men in front of the house. Somewhere a lark began to sing. "Get ready," Sam whispered hoarsely into the front room.

Sam peeked from a corner of the window he had shattered when he dove through it. Shadowy figures began emerging from the barn, the stable, the bunkhouse. Others left the corral. Around front, more men stepped from behind the shade trees that had been planted around the house or raised themselves out of the high grass. They moved toward the house, rifles ready. Most were dressed like cowboys, a few like townsmen. "Can't nobody be alive in there after all that," Sam heard one of them boast. Sam looked for Chandler or Branko but did not see them, and he swore softly. Those were the ones he wanted in his rifle sights.

Sam let Chandler's men get close. He hoped Jack was paying attention on the other side. Then he poked the rifle barrel through the broken window. He fired, dropping a man outside the house. The others froze. Sam levered and fired, dropping another. Confused, Chandler's men fired back, but they made perfect targets. When Sam hit a third, they ran. They got back to the buildings and opened fire again, turning the ranch house into kindling. Men ran from the bunkhouse and dragged their hit comrades back under cover. Sam didn't fire at them. Somehow it didn't seem right.

As Sam opened fire in the back room, Jack went into action out front. The closest men to him were two who had emerged from the cotton-woods planted on the eastern side of the house. As Sam began shooting out back, the two men froze in surprise. At that moment Jack stepped through the door with the shotgun. Moving toward the men, he discharged first one barrel, then the other, and the two men were blown nearly in half at point-blank range. Jack pulled his pistol and fired at the other men in the open, who were now shooting at him. A bullet grazed his ribs and he cried out. He pulled himself back into the house and slammed the door behind him. He took his rifle and began firing at the rest of Chandler's men, who retreated in confusion.

The gunfire on the house resumed. The horses in the barn had calmed down; either they were exhausted or they had grown used to the noise. A stray bullet killed a chicken wandering across the backyard, and some of Chandler's men sent up a derisive cheer.

Sam crawled into the front room, where Jack was bandaging his side with strips torn from his shirt. "You all right?" Sam asked him.

"Yeah," Jack replied. He was sober now, but his tongue was thick from last night's whiskey and it was hard for him to talk. "All this shooting is giving me a godawful headache. I'm thirsty, too. I wish there was some water in the house."

Sam didn't feel sorry for him. "I wouldn't mind a drink myself, but I don't think Chandler is going to let us use the well. If it makes you feel better, Chandler will have to do something soon. All this gunfire is likely to attract attention. If Chandler and his men stay here much longer, some of your friends are going to show up. They may have said they'll quit, but my guess is they won't back away from a straight-up fight like this one."

Outside, the firing stopped. From the tall grass in front of the house, Chandler's voice called, "Slater? Mitchell?"

"What do you want, Chandler?" Sam shouted back.

"I want you to give up. We have Lucinda."

Sam and Jack exchanged looks. "Prove it," called Jack.

There was a pause, then Lucinda's voice cried, "Sam! Jack! Don't . . ." There was a muffled noise as she was cut off.

"Proof enough?" Chandler shouted. "Now come out, or we'll kill her."

Jack slumped, defeated. He started to get

up, but Sam grabbed his arm, holding him down. "Go ahead," he called to Chandler.

"What!" said Chandler.

"You heard me. Go ahead and kill her, if that's what you want."

Jack flared at Sam. "Are you . . . ?"

"He won't do it," Sam told him. "He loves her."

In front of the house, Chandler held Lucinda's arms and seethed. Branko stood nearby, reloading his rifle. Tom Singer was there, too, looking guilty and out of place.

Lucinda turned to her captor with a mixture of mockery and triumph. "Well? What are you going to do now?"

"I'll show you," Chandler swore. He beckoned to Branko.

Sam became aware of activity inside the barn. Soon a group of Chandler's men pushed out a wagon loaded with hay. Sam swore; he knew what was coming. Gunfire redoubled on the house, preventing Sam from getting a shot at the men around the wagon.

One of Chandler's men struck a match to the hay. They waited until it was burning good. In the front room Jack smelled the fire, and he turned up at Sam's elbow. "What's going on?" he asked, taking a quick peek out the window.

"It's called a 'go-down,'" Sam told him. "You can guess what it's for."

As he spoke a group of Chandler's men began to push the burning wagon toward the house.

CHAPTER 21

THE WAGON LOADED WITH BURNING HAY
rumbled closer. Bullets spattered into the house
walls and knocked what was left of the shutters
and the glass behind them out of the windows.
Ignoring the danger, Sam began shooting at the
men pushing the wagon. "Come on," he told
Jack, "unless you want to be the main course at
your own barbecue."

Jack took the other rear window and joined in. A
bullet gouged the sill by Sam's head, and a splinter
tore through his scarred cheek. Another bullet
clipped Jack's earlobe, causing blood to pour over
his shoulder. They paid no attention, but kept firing.

One of the men pushing the wagon grabbed his knee and fell. That threw the others off stride, but by now it was too late. The wagon was close; it had developed a momentum of its own. With a last push, Chandler's men sent it on its way and stood back.

"Look out!" Sam yelled.

He and Jack jumped out of the way as the burning wagon crashed into the rear of the house. The heavy vehicle broke halfway through the wall before becoming stuck in place. The flames from the burning hay threw off intense heat and smoke. The dry frame of the walls caught fire almost immediately. Tongues of flame licked in all directions.

Sam and Jack grabbed blankets and table-cloths and beat at the flames, trying to extin-guish them, choking and coughing in the smoke. It was no use. The flames spread more rapidly than they could be put out. The roof took fire now, as well. Sparks flew, spreading the blaze still further.

In the smoke Jack couldn't breathe. He was beaten up and hungover, dehydrated from all the alcohol in his system. It was hard for him to keep driving his body. His head felt like it was ready to explode, and the heat made it worse. His tongue was so swollen from thirst that he thought it would choke him. He panicked and ran for the front door.

Sam grabbed Jack's waist, stopping him. "No!" Sam said.

Jack was bug eyed. "We've got to get out!"

"That's what Chandler wants," Sam shouted above the roar of the flames. "He and his men will be waiting for us."

Jack tried to pull out of Sam's grasp. "That's all right. I'll take my chances out there."

"No, I said."

"What do you want to do, be burned alive?"

Sam tried to think, with the fire consuming the house around him. Then he had an idea. In Jack's ear he yelled, "Find everything that will burn. Throw it on the fire."

Jack stared at him. "You're . . ."

"Do it!" Sam said, giving him a push.

Sam kicked open the front door, both to provide air for the fire and to give the smoke a way of escaping. The two men dragged the mattresses from the beds and threw them on the fire. They pulled up the rugs and threw them on as well, followed by the tablecloths, blankets, and all the spare clothes. Then came the furniture—Jack's chair exploded when his whiskey jugs hit the flames. Sam and Jack drew bandannas over their faces as protection from the smoke; they shielded themselves from the heat with their arms. They were black from powder smoke, and the intense heat and sweat that the fire generated made the powder blacking run down their faces like slurry.

The house was rapidly stripped of combustibles. Sam saw the Mitchells' Bible open on the floor. He picked it up and started to toss it onto the blaze, but Jack took it out of his hand. "No! I won't have you destroying the Good Book."

Sam wasn't going to fight about it. "Have it your way." Jack slipped the Bible into his shirt.

Outside, Lucinda watched the flames engulf her house and the two men she loved. Smoke billowed through the windows and the open door. In a thick cloud it drifted down on her and the men around her. It stung their eyes and made breathing difficult. The smell of burning wood and cloth was heavy in the air.

All around, Chandler's men fingered their rifles, waiting for Sam and Jack to emerge. Some of them pulled up their bandannas because of the smoke. In desperation Lucinda turned to Chandler. "Do something, can't you?"

"It's too late now," Chandler told her.

In the house the heat had reached furnace-level intensity. Everything that would burn had been thrown on the fire. Flames were all around. The roof would go any minute. Smoke roiled out the door in grayish clouds, spreading over the front of the house, driven by the northwest wind right into the faces of Chandler and the men with him, as Sam had intended.

Sam felt his hair and shirt singe. His blackened skin was blistering. Jack was just as bad.

"Lie down," Sam ordered.

As if drugged, Jack did as he was told. Smoke rose, and what little air remained in the house was just above the floor. Jack fought to keep from passing out.

"Got your rifle?" Sam asked.

Jack coughed. "Yeah."

Sam leaned in close. He could hardly breathe, and the smoke stung his eyes so badly that he kept them partway closed. He yelled hoarsely in Jack's ear. "Follow me. Keep low to the ground. We're going to try and sneak out in the smoke. Maybe they won't see us. It's our only chance."

Jack nodded weakly.

"Come on." Sam started crawling for the door. Behind him part of the roof fell with a flaming crash. The smoke was so thick he couldn't see a thing. He only hoped that Chandler and his men were having the same problem. The draft led him to the door. Jack was right behind, now and then reaching ahead and touching Sam's heel to make sure he was still going the right way.

Then Sam was out the door. The thick

smoke was spreading all over the landscape. To his left Sam heard part of the gallery and one of its supports fall. "Keep going," he told Jack behind him. He found the edge of the porch and let himself drop off it into the dirt. He followed the course of the drifting smoke, hoping to make the tall grass. If they got that far, they had a chance.

Outside the house, Chandler and his men moved back, afraid that the fire's growing heat would explode the cartridges in their guns and on their shell belts. Smoke billowed over them like thick fog, making it impossible for them to see the ranch house's front door. Part of the roof had gone, and now the rest collapsed in a shower of sparks and flame, dimly perceived through the smoke.

"What do you think?" Branko said, coughing, to Chandler. "Are they dead?"

"I didn't hear any screams," Chandler replied. His eyes had been turned into slits by the heat and smoke. He averted his face from the burning house.

"Maybe the smoke got them first," Branko suggested.

Nearby, young Tom Singer said, "Can't be nobody left alive in there."

Chandler said, "Just keep watching that

door, damn it. Those two are capable of anything, especially that bastard Slater."

Lucinda looked up at the cattleman. "You rotten, murdering . . ." Her voice tailed off—sad, weary, hopeless.

Chandler said, "It's just you and me now, Lucinda."

Lucinda's face filled with shock and loathing. "I wouldn't have you if you were the last man on earth."

"As far as you're concerned, I am."

"What do you mean?"

"You don't think I'm going to let you go, do you? Not after this. And I'd never kill you. No, Lucinda, you're going to stay with me. Now, and for always."

She took a step back. "You're insane. You could never get away with that."

Chandler smiled grimly. "You'd be surprised what you can get away with in this country, if you have enough money."

Because of the thick smoke, Sam and Jack were in the tall grass that grew in front of the ranch house before they knew that they had reached it. They lay with their faces in the dirt, exhausted, their oxygen-starved lungs heaving and choking from their effort, trying not to make noise.

After a second, Sam raised up. "Come on," he told Jack.

Jack's look was pained. "You mean, keep going?"

"We're not safe here. We're too close to the house. This smoke'll blow over soon, and we'll be sitting ducks."

"How far do we have to go?"

"As far as we can. Across the stream, anyway, then find a place to hole up till Chandler and his men leave. With luck they'll think we're dead and they won't look around too hard."

They crawled on, hidden by the grass now as well as the smoke, but trying not to disturb the grass, lest the waving stalks betray their presence. The gray-black smoke hung over everything, like a funeral pall. Soot drifted down on the two men as they inched their way along, each movement taking them farther away from Chandler's men and closer to safety.

The ranch house collapsed upon itself, leaving a pile of flaming ruins. Lucinda could no longer pretend there was any hope for Sam and Jack. Half blinded by the smoke, she hung her head and cried. Nearby, Chandler viewed the destruction with a look of triumph. This was the moment for which he had waited so long. The Arrowhead Basin was all his. Next to him, Branko felt cheated at not having been able to settle with Sam Slater himself—and collect the reward on Slater's head. Behind them, Tom Singer looked like he wanted to be sick.

After a tortuous crawl, Sam and Jack reached the stream. Both men were racked by thirst. Sam scooped a few handfuls of water into his mouth and kept going. Only his Apache training and discipline kept him from lying there and drinking until he was surfeited. Beyond the need to get away, it was too dangerous to remain in the open area by the stream. Sam crawled into the icy water, raising his rifle and shell belt above the surface with one hand.

Behind him Jack was all in. He lay on the sandy bank with his face in the water, drinking. His dehydrated body cried out for liquid. He couldn't get enough of it.

Sam hissed and beckoned him forward, but Jack paid no attention. He kept drinking.

Sam raised his voice urgently. "Come on!"

"All right," Jack mumbled. He lay his head on the sand for a second, to ease the pulsing pain and to collect his strength. He didn't see why they couldn't stay here. Surely they had gone far enough?

Then, through the haze, he became aware of something lying near him. He turned his head a bit more and saw his big yellow dog, Vic. The dog's head was at the edge of the water that it had tried so desperately to reach. Its eyes were open, its lips peeled back in a rictus of poisoned death, revealing its teeth and heavy globs of dried drool on its protruding tongue and chin.

"Oh, shit!" said Jack out loud. Involuntarily he moved away from the dead dog, half rising to his feet as he did.

Even as he realized his mistake and dropped back to the ground, there came a startled cry from behind him.

"Hey—there they are!"

CHAPTER 22

SAM JUMPED TO HIS FEET. "RUN, YOU FOOL!" he told Jack. Still carrying the rifle and shell belt, he started running himself, across the stream and into the long grass on the other side.

Jack scrambled up behind him. He splashed clumsily across the stream on his tired legs. His gait was unsteady; he had a hard time keeping his feet. The ice-cold water took his breath away, hindering him still further. Behind them were yells and gunshots.

* * *

Not far away, Clay Chandler watched the two men fleeing through the long grass. He couldn't believe what he saw.

"How could they have gotten away?" said Branko beside him.

Lucinda stepped forward. "Run, Sam! Run, Jack!"

Chandler grabbed her and pulled her back, then he turned to his men. "Don't stand there, get after them. On your horses, you men."

Sam and Jack ran. Sam was looking for some kind of cover, some place to make a stand—a place to make the dying take a bit longer. They ran with their heads down, bullets whispering through the air around them, searching them out. Sam cursed Jack for giving them away, then realized he was being too hard on him. Chandler's men would have spotted them eventually. It never had been much of a chance.

Then Sam saw what he had been looking for—a cutback about a hundred yards off. It would give them cover on one side. It was as good as they were going to get. He heard horses now. Chandler's men were riding around them, cutting off their retreat.

Behind Sam, Jack was panting. He stumbled to a stop, heaving for breath. "I can't . . . can't go on."

Sam hesitated. He took a last look at the cut-back, then started back toward Jack. Hell, he thought, one place is as good to die as another.

Sam reached Jack, who was bent over, pain and exhaustion on his face. Both men were blistered and blackened, their clothes half burned off. As Sam buckled his shell belt on again, he and Jack stood back to back, watching Chandler's gunmen coming toward them in the tall grass, while other men surrounded them on horseback.

"Now I know how Custer felt," muttered Jack.

They knelt, to present less of a target. With his rifle Sam drew a bead and picked off one of the riders, who pitched from his saddle into the grass.

"That'll make them keep their distance," Sam said. "For a few minutes, anyway."

Chandler's men were quick learners. The riders dismounted; the others went to ground. They had Sam and Jack surrounded and they began shooting, pouring in fire from all directions. Sam and Jack returned the fire as best they could. In the distance, Sam saw Lucinda. She was crying, trying to come to them, with Chandler holding her back.

Around them the stalks of the long grass were clipped and clipped again. The humming bullets sounded like a nest of disturbed bees.

Sam saw dust spurt from Jack's side. Jack fell to one hand, but steadied himself. Sam saw a hole in his shirt, but no blood.

"What the . . . ?" Sam said.

Jack reached into his shirt and pulled out his thick Bible, which had a large bullet hole in its leather cover. "I told you not to destroy the Good Book," he said.

"Praise the Lord," said Sam.

Sam turned back to the fight. As he did, a bullet struck the receiver of his rifle, smashing it and knocking the weapon from his hands. Sam's right hand stung; he shook it. A quick look told him that the Winchester was no longer operable. He drew his pistol.

"You all right?" asked Jack.

"Yeah." Sam paused, watching the field around him. "How are you fixed for ammunition?"

"I been fixed better."

The two men held their fire. They had too few shells left; they could only afford to spend bullets on good targets. Besides, Sam wasn't going to hit anybody with the pistol unless they were right on top of him.

"Lay low," Sam told Jack. "Wait for them to make their move. We'll take a few of them with us."

Sam and Jack crouched down. Sam was still waiting for Jack to apologize for the way he'd treated him, and still no apology came. Sam guessed it didn't make much difference now.

They heard Chandler's men crunching the grass, moving in for the kill. "Here they come," Sam whispered.

The noises came closer. Sam got ready to spring to his feet and get off a few rounds before the hurricane of gunfire cut him down.

Then Sam heard distant gunshots, from downstream. Chandler's men stopped and looked behind them. The gunshots grew louder; there was the sound of horses, coming hard.

Sam raised up and looked. "It's your friends," he told Jack.

There were about fifteen of them in all—big Mike Kennedy, Sid Allison, Boyer, Biscuit, Phil, the others. They rode in firing pistols and rifles, angry and at the same time eager to finally have an enemy they could see.

Chandler's men were surprised and caught in the open. This was not the kind of fight they had expected, or liked. For a few minutes they put up a stiff resistance. The crack of rifles and popping of revolvers sounded across the range. Men fell on both sides. Then Sam and Jack joined in the fight from the gunmen's rear, and Chandler's men began to melt away. Those with horses climbed on them and rode for safety. Those on foot ran back for their mounts. Some were shot and fell, others dropped their weapons and threw up their hands in surrender. A few reached their tethered horses and mounted up.

Clay Chandler was furious. "Stand and fight!" he yelled at his men. But they ignored him. They were paid to kill, not to die themselves. Chandler looked around. Everyone was deserting him. Even Branko had pulled out, so stealthily that Chandler had not noticed him leaving.

Nearby Tom Singer mounted, terrified lest his friends catch him with Chandler. As he swung his leg over the horse's back, a bullet hit him. He paused, then toppled backward, with his left foot caught in the stirrup. The frightened horse ran off, dragging Tom's body across the ground.

Lucinda took advantage of Chandler's distraction to twist away from him and run. Chandler went after her. He caught her and grabbed her around the neck with his forearm. He tried to drag her back and unhitch the horses from the cottonwood tree to which they were tied, but it was hard to do while holding the struggling Lucinda.

Sam and Jack ran up, weapons leveled. Some of the other small ranchers were there, too. Scattered gunfire still sounded, but it was dying down. Chandler held his pistol to Lucinda's head and cocked it. "Don't come any closer," he warned.

Sam and Jack stopped. "You won't do it," Sam told Chandler.

"This time I will," Chandler assured him. "Believe me, if it comes down to her or me, I'll pick me every time."

Sam and Jack said nothing. Sam's chest heaved with anger. He wanted to shoot, but Chandler could pull the trigger before he moved. The slightest movement could make the cocked pistol go off.

Chandler went on, "All of you, put down your guns. I want two horses—now—or little Miss Lucinda here goes to meet her ancestors. I've got nothing to lose, gentlemen. You can kill me, but you'll kill her, too. It's your call."

Reluctantly, Sam lay his pistol on the ground. "Go head, boys. Do as he says." Jack and the others put down their weapons, as well. The pudgy cowboy named Biscuit dismounted and untied Chandler's horses.

At that moment Lucinda wrenched Chandler's arm away from her neck, and she sank her teeth deep into his wrist.

"Ow!" yelled Chandler. With a violent effort, he shook her loose, knocking her to the ground.

Before he could grab her again, Sam dove for his pistol and fired. The bullet struck Chandler in the chest. Chandler took a couple steps backward. He tried to raise his own pistol, but Sam fired again, and again. Chandler swayed, then fell forward on his face.

Lucinda was on the ground, crying. As she rose, Jack ran up and embraced her. "Are you all right?" he asked.

"Yes, yes," she said. "They didn't hurt me."

Sam kicked the pistol away from Chandler's hand. He knelt and checked Chandler.

"Is he dead?" asked the bearded rancher Kennedy, coming up.

Sam nodded. Then he said, "You boys happened along just in time."

"We heard the gunfire. Hell, you could hear it all over the Basin. Sounded like Gettysburg all over again." Kennedy paused, clearing his throat awkwardly. "You know, Slater, I guess . . . I guess me and the others was wrong about you."

"Forget it," Sam told him.

Lucinda broke away from Jack. She came to Sam, who put an arm around her while she cried on his shoulder. "I thought you and Jack were dead," she said.

"So did I," Sam admitted.

All around, the ranchers were rounding up what was left of Chandler's men and bringing them in. "What should we do with them?" Kennedy asked Sam.

"Let 'em go. They're no threat now that Chandler is dead. All they'll want to do is get out of here as quick as they can." He looked around, "Speaking of which—where is Branko?"

"He got away," Lucinda said.

Sam walked over to Chandler's horse. Chandler's rifle was still in its saddle bucket. To Kennedy, Sam said, "Give me some .44–40 shells, will you?"

Kennedy obliged. "What are you going to do?"

Sam reloaded his pistol, then he unhitched the horse and mounted. "I'm going after Branko. I don't think Chandler will mind if I borrow his horse, do you?"

CHAPTER 23

BRANKO PESIC LET HIS HORSE PICK ITS WAY along the narrow hill trail. It was chilly here in the hills, shaded as they were by thick spruce and ponderosa pine, along with stands of aspen from which the golden leaves were falling. It reminded Branko of the forested mountains near his home town of Priština. Except for the presence of this horse he might almost have been at home. He sighed at that thought, then shifted uncomfortably in the saddle. He would be terribly sore by the time he reached Bannack or Virginia City—whichever destination he decided on—but at least he would be getting there in one piece, and with money in his pockets.

After leaving the Mitchell ranch, Branko had ridden to the head of the Mitchells' valley. The rest of Chandler's surviving men had turned off for Buffalo Notch. Branko had elected to work his way northwest through these rugged hills. If all went well, he would camp tonight at Lake McKenzie, then leave the Basin tomorrow by its northern end. This route was more difficult, but it was also less likely that he'd be caught by the vengeful ranchers. Nobody would be expecting him to come this way. Nobody had even seen him leave.

He sighed again. This job with Chandler had turned into a complete balls-up at the end—just when Chandler had seemed on the verge of total success. If it hadn't been for that meddling Slater, Jack Mitchell would have been hung from one of his own cottonwoods this morning, and the Arrowhead Basin would have belonged to Chandler.

Oh, well, Branko thought, no one could blame *him* for what had happened. He had done his part. He was particularly proud of the way he had silenced Mitchell's watchdogs. He had learned the trick of the poisoned meat while working for a gang of Obrenovich assassins at home, where political opponents routinely kept fierce dogs for protection. If Chandler's "gunmen" had been better shots, things might not have ended this way, but it was too late to worry. Branko had gotten out with his life; he would soon find work again.

He planned to remain at one of the mining camps through the winter, then perhaps head for San Francisco in the spring. Even in far-off Serbia they had heard of the fabulously wealthy San Francisco. People said it was built on hills, like ancient Rome. A man with Branko's talents should do well there.

As Branko rounded a bend in the wooded trail, he stopped. There was another rider on the trail waiting for him, pistol drawn. The rider was tall and lean. His skin was burned and blistered; what remained of his clothing was covered with dried blood. The wide brim of his hat shaded his eyes, but Branko could see a fearsome scar along his torn and bleeding left cheek.

"Slater," said Branko.

One corner of Sam's mouth lifted in an ironic smile. "You weren't exactly hard to trail, Branko. If you were trying to cover your tracks, you did a piss-poor job of it. Once I got behind you, I figured which way you were going. I still know these hills pretty well, so it was easy to get ahead of you. As a matter of fact, you took so long getting here, I was afraid you had gotten lost."

"Perhaps I should have gotten lost," Branko

said, "considering the circumstances in which I now find myself. What do you intend?"

Sam motioned with the pistol. "Get off your horse."

The small man shrugged and did as he was told. His horse wandered off among the trees. Then Sam dismounted as well. He holstered his pistol.

Branko raised his thick eyebrows in surprise.

Sam said, "Like I told your late boss, I never kill a man without giving him a chance."

Branko smiled. "I think you have made a big mistake, Mister Slater."

"Let's find out, shall we?" Sam stood easy, hand resting near his pistol. "Ready when you are."

Branko set himself. He went for his gun.

Sam had his pistol drawn and cocked before Branko's weapon was even level. Branko swallowed in disbelief.

"Don't stop now," Sam told him.

Suddenly Branko tossed his pistol to the ground, smiling broadly. "I surrender," he announced.

Sam's eyes narrowed.

Branko was cheerful now, ebullient. "Yes, I give up. Go ahead, you may take me in. Lock me up. Certainly, I killed Singer and Pratt. I killed that fool Fleming and a number of others, as well. So try and convict me of it. I have money locked away in Deadwood—enough to hire the best lawyers. You have no evidence, and I doubt there are any witnesses left to testify against me. You will not be able to convict me of anything more than killing those dogs. I will be a free man before the snow falls. So go ahead, mister bounty hunter, take me in." His big smile widened still further.

Sam fired his pistol.

Branko's smile turned into a look of surprise. Blood leaked out of a small hole above his heart. He swayed on his feet for a moment, then he twisted and fell on his back, his lifeless eyes staring at the sky.

"Wrong answer," Sam said.

CHAPTER 24

THE SUN WAS WELL INTO THE WEST WHEN Sam returned to the Mitchell ranch. He brought Branko's horse with him. He had left Branko's body where it lay. It had not been worth burying.

The ranch house was a burnt-out ruin. A few wisps of smoke still rose from the charred embers. The only bit of good fortune was that the prevailing wind had blown the sparks away from the other ranch buildings, which remained intact.

Jack and Lucinda were the only ones left at the ranch. They had let the horses into the corral to exercise, and right now they were cleaning up the battlefield, removing shell casings along with discarded weapons and articles of clothing.

They stopped what they were doing as Sam approached. Jack was tired; there were dark circles under his eyes. He had washed up some, but wore the same clothes—his others had been destroyed in the fire. The bandage around his ribs was dirty; there was dried blood on his shoulder from the shot-away earlobe. Lucinda was dirty but otherwise all right. Strands of her black hair had come unpinned and hung alongside her face.

"Where's Branko?" asked Jack as Sam climbed off Chandler's horse.

"Dead," Sam said. "Where did everybody go?"

Lucinda answered. "The ranchers took the wounded and the prisoners to Buffalo Notch. We had three dead, who were removed to their homes. There will be a prayer service for them here tomorrow. Afterwards, there's going to be a house-raising for us."

"We're going to build her up bigger and better than ever," Jack said proudly. Jack's entire whiskey supply must have been consumed in the fire; this was the first time Sam had seen him sober.

"What about Chandler's dead?" Sam asked.

Jack motioned. "They're buried across the creek, along with Chandler, in an unmarked grave."

Sadly, Lucinda added, "Except for Clay, no one knew their names, or whether they had families back in Texas, or wherever it was they came from. Now, I guess no one ever will."

"The threat to the Basin is gone," Jack said. "Now we can hold our roundup and throw together a trail herd—realize some money from this year's work. The other ranchers will stay now, new settlers will come in. There's great times ahead."

Sam loosened the saddle girths on the two horses. "And Chandler's ranch?"

Lucinda said, "It will be broken up, I guess, sold in lots. The same with his herd. It will provide a lot of work for the lawyers."

Sam nodded, and Lucinda went on. "What about you, Sam? Have you decided whether to stay on here? Say you will, please."

Sam let out his breath and looked around at the sweeping vista of rangeland and mountain. "You know, this country's the closest thing I've ever had to a real home."

Lucinda was persuasive. "There's a great opportunity here now, Sam. With Chandler and so many of the ranchers gone, there's plenty of prime rangeland to be had. Plus, half the S Bar S is yours. We all want you to stay."

Sam wrinkled his brow in thought. Then he smiled at Lucinda. He was about to reply, when he heard the sound of hoofbeats.

The three of them turned to see the bearded rancher Mike Kennedy coming on hell for leather, lashing his horse with his reins's ends. His hat had blown back on his head and was only held on by its chin strap.

"Now what?" muttered Jack.

Kennedy thundered across the stream in a spray of water. He pulled up and dismounted in one movement, out of breath. "Slater," he gasped, "that U.S. Marshal from Helena is here. He's raised a big posse in Buffalo Notch and he's coming this way, after you. Me and the boys ran into them while we were taking the wounded to town. I circled around 'em to get back here and warn you. They can't be more than ten minutes behind me."

Lucinda grabbed Sam's arm. "This doesn't change a thing, Sam. We'll get the charge against you dismissed, like we talked about before."

Kennedy shook his head. "The marshal's got you on four more counts. He's charging you with the deaths of Marshal Cummings and his men. He don't look like he's in a mood to listen to reason, neither. I tried to explain what happened, but he didn't want to hear it."

Sam took Lucinda's shoulders. Quietly he said, "I have to go, Lucy. I'll need a horse."

She understood, and her face fell. "I'll get one."

While Sam fetched his saddle and trail gear

from the barn, Lucinda led Honeysuckle from the corral. Sam looked at her with surprise. "Lucy, this is your horse."

"Take him," she said. "He's the fastest in the Basin."

"Lucy, I can't . . ."

She stamped her foot. "Sam Slater, I order you to take him."

"Better hurry," Kennedy told them, looking back downstream.

Sam hesitated, then he threw his bridle and saddle on Honeysuckle. As he was tying on his blanket roll, he had a funny feeling.

"Sam!" screamed Lucy.

Sam dropped to the ground, rolling and drawing his pistol. There was a shot, and a bullet hit the ground where he had been. Lying on his back, he raised his pistol and fired twice at Jack, hitting him both times.

Jack dropped his own pistol. He fell to his hands and knees and began vomiting blood from his mouth and nose. Lucinda stared, distraught. Kennedy couldn't believe what had happened. Sam raised himself slowly from the ground, heart racing.

Jack fell onto his side. His face was suddenly pale. Bright red blood covered the lower part of his face and the front of his shirt. Sam knelt and rested Jack's head on his leg. To Kennedy he said, "Get some water."

Jack shook his head impatiently. "No time," he said, and he coughed up more blood. He reached up and grabbed Sam's sleeve. "Have to . . . have to tell you. I was . . . one who sent to Helena for marshal."

"You!" said Lucinda.

Jack nodded. "Told him you were here. Told Marshal Cummings, too." He caught his breath. "Those times you were shot at? It was me. Even that first time. Knew it was you when I spotted you coming through the Notch that day."

"Why?" Sam asked him. "Why did you do it? Was it for the reward?"

Jack shook his head and coughed up bloody froth. There was a rattling sound in his throat, like pebbles in a tin can. He smiled wanly, beckoning Sam closer. Sam leaned in and Jack whispered to him. "To get rid of the ghosts."

Then Jack let out a long, shuddering sigh and fell back, dead.

Sam let Jack's body down gently. He stood and looked at Lucinda. He held out his hands in a gesture of apology, and they were covered with her husband's blood. "That's the second time I've killed the man in your life, Lucy. I didn't want to do it. It was self-defense, just like before."

From behind them Kennedy yelled, "Here they come! I see their dust!"

Downstream, a dust cloud showed where the marshal's posse was coming on fast.

Lucinda pushed Honeysuckle's reins into Sam's hand. "Go, Sam. They'll be here any minute."

"But . . . what about you? What about the ranch? How will you run it by yourself?"

"I'll manage," she said, and tears rolled down her cheeks. "Just like before."

They could hear the heavy rumble of the posse's hoofbeats now. "Hurry," urged Lucy. "Save yourself."

Sam bent and kissed Lucinda's forehead. "Goodbye, Lucy."

She hugged him and kissed his cheek in return. "Goodbye, Sam."

Sam swung onto Honeysuckle and gathered the reins in his hand. He gave Lucinda a last look, then he wheeled the horse and rode off.

Just like before.

Dale Colter is the pseudonym of a full-time writer who lives in Maryland with his family.

HarperPaperbacks *By Mail*

ZANE GREY CLASSICS

THE DUDE RANGER
0-06-100055-8 $3.50

THE LOST WAGON TRAIN
0-06-100064-7 $3.99

WILDFIRE
0-06-100081-7 $3.50

THE MAN OF THE FOREST
0-06-100082-5 $3.95

THE BORDER LEGION
0-06-100083-3 $3.95

SUNSET PASS
0-06-100084-1 $3.50

30,000 ON HOOF
0-06-100085-X $3.50

THE WANDERER OF THE WASTELAND
0-06-100092-2 $3.50

TWIN SOMBREROS
0-06-100101-5 $3.50

BOULDER DAM
0-06-100111-2 $3.50

THE TRAIL DRIVER
0-06-100154-6 $3.50

TO THE LAST MAN
0-06-100218-6 $3.50

THUNDER MOUNTAIN
0-06-100216-X $3.50

THE CODE OF THE WEST
0-06-100173-2 $3.50

ARIZONA AMES
0-06-100171-6 $3.50

ROGUE RIVER FEUD
0-06-100214-3 $3.95

THE THUNDERING HERD
0-06-100217-8 $3.95

HORSE HEAVEN HILL
0-06-100210-0 $3.95

Saddle-up to these

THE REGULATOR by Dale Colter
Sam Slater, blood brother of the Apache
and a cunning bounty-hunter, is out to
collect the big price on the heads of the
murderous Pauley gang. He'll give them
a single choice: surrender and live, or go
for your sixgun.

THE REGULATOR—Diablo At Daybreak
by Dale Colter
The Governor wants the blood of the
Apache murderers who ravaged his
daughter. He gives Sam Slater a choice:
work for him, or face a noose. Now
Slater must hunt down the deadly rene-
gade Chacon...Slater's Apache brother.

THE JUDGE by Hank Edwards
Federal Judge Clay Torn is more than a
judge—sometimes he has to be the jury
and the executioner. Torn pits himself
against the most violent and ruthless
man in Kansas, a battle whose final ver-
dict will judge one man right...and one
man dead.

THE JUDGE—War Clouds
by Hank Edwards
Judge Clay Torn rides into Dakota where
the Cheyenne are painting for war and
the army is shining steel and loading
lead. If war breaks out, someone is
going to make a pile of money on a river
of blood.

If you would like to receive a HarperPaperbacks
catalog, fill out the coupon below and send $1.00
postage/handling to:

HarperPaperbacks Catalog Request
10 East 53rd St.
New York, NY 10022

Name _____

Address _____

State _____ Zip _____